EMBASSY SIEGE

SAS
OPERATION

Embassy Siege

SHAUN CLARKE

HARPER

Harper
An imprint of HarperCollins*Publishers*
1 London Bridge Street,
London SE1 9GF
www.harpercollins.co.uk

This paperback edition 2016
1

First published by 22 Books/Bloomsbury Publishing plc 1994

Copyright © Bloomsbury Publishing plc 1994

Shaun Clarke asserts the moral right to
be identified as the author of this work

A catalogue record for this book
is available from the British Library

ISBN: 978 0 00 815512 4

Set in Sabon by Born Group using Atomik ePublisher from Easypress

Printed and bound in Great Britain

MIX
Paper from
responsible sources
FSC **FSC® C007454**
www.fsc.org

Prelude

Number 16 Princes Gate formed part of a mid-Victorian terrace overlooking Hyde Park and had been used as the Iranian Embassy in London for more than a decade. Until 1979, it had represented the Iran ruled by Shah Reza Pahlavi and his wife, the Empress Fara Diba.

Noted for its Italianate stucco façade and prominent frieze, it was a very large building spread over three main floors and an attic. The ground floor comprised an imposing entrance hall, a large, beautifully furnished reception room, toilets, an administration office, and an expansive library overlooking the rear terrace. The main stairs led up to the first floor and the rather grand ambassador's office, the more modest office of the chargé d'affaires, two administration offices and a storage room. The second floor contained two more administration offices, Rooms 9, 9A and 10, another toilet and a telex room. The third floor was the busiest, containing the press counsellor's office, the press room, the commercial office, the xerox room, the switchboard, Room 19, the kitchen, a toilet, and two more administration rooms, one of which was empty. A well skylight with a glass roof, located between Room 19, the switchboard, the xerox room and the outer wall, overlooked the main stairs connecting the three floors. As the lift terminated on the second floor, the third floor could only be reached by the stairs.

When run by the Shah's young and eligible Ambassador, Parvis Radji, the Embassy had been noted for its lavish dinner parties and largesse when it came to supplying excellent caviar, French wines, cars, free hotels and first-class travel to British diplomats, journalists and other visitors whose goodwill and assistance were vital to Iran. However, while ostentatiously maintaining this front of gracious, civilized living, the Embassy had also been used as a base for SAVAK, the Shah's dreaded secret police, whose function was to spy on and intimidate London-based Iranians, mostly students. Many of these secret police were uneducated, unsophisticated and addicted to the Western 'decadence' they were supposed to despise: nightclubs, alcohol and bought women.

Such activities had, however, ended with the downfall of the Shah in January 1979. Six months after the revolution, the Ayatollahs replaced Parvis Radji with a new chargé d'affaires, Dr Ali Afrouz, a twenty-nine-year-old graduate in psychology and education. Once installed in the Embassy at Princes Gate, Ali weeded out the corrupt members of SAVAK, banned all alcohol from the premises, got rid of the more ostentatious luxuries of the previous regime, and in general ensured that Embassy business was conducted in a more modest, formal manner.

In the days of the Shah, the Embassy's front door had been guarded by the British security company Securicor. Unfortunately, when Dr Afrouz took over, he dropped the company and gave the job to an Iranian, Abbas Fallahi, who had been the Embassy's butler and knew precious little about security.

More knowledgeable in this area was Police Constable Trevor Lock, at that time a member of the Diplomatic

Protection Group. This organization, being unable to give individual protection to each of London's 138 embassies and High Commissions, was based at several strategic points in West London, remained constantly on alert in case of emergency, and also provided individual armed guards as part of the British Government's token contribution to the embassies' security.

Though not due to serve at the Iranian Embassy that morning, PC Lock agreed to stand in for a colleague who required the day off for personal matters. So it was that at approximately 1100 on 30 April, the policeman strapped his holstered standard-police issue .38 Smith and Wesson revolver to his thigh, carefully buttoned his tunic over the holster, then set out for the Embassy.

One of the most loyal members of the Embassy staff was not an Iranian, but an Englishman, Ron Morris, who had joined as an office boy twenty-five years before, when he was only fourteen. Ron had graduated to the position of chauffeur, then, when the luxuries of the Shah's days were swept away, among them the ambassadorial Rolls-Royce Silver Ghost, he was made a caretaker and general maintenance man.

Just before nine o'clock on the morning of 30 April, Ron bid a routine farewell to his Italian wife Maria and cat Gingerella, left his basement flat in Chester Street, Belgravia, and drove on his moped to the Embassy, arriving there on the dot of nine. After parking his moped against the railings, he entered the building and began work as usual.

Two hours later, Simeon 'Sim' Harris, a thirty-three-year-old sound recordist, and Chris Cramer, a thirty-one-year-old news organizer, both with the BBC and widely experienced in the world's trouble spots, arrived at the Embassy to try yet again – they had tried and failed before – to obtain visas to visit

Iran. They were met by the doorman, Abbas Fallahi, who led them to the reception room, located through the first door on the left in the entrance hall. While waiting there, they were joined by another visitor, Ali Tabatabai, an employee of Iran's Bank Markazi. In London for a fourteen-week course for international bankers run by the Midland Bank, Ali was visiting the Embassy to collect a film and map of Iran for a talk he was to give as part of his course. He sat beside the two BBC men and, like them, waited patiently.

These three visitors were soon joined by Majtaba Mehrnavard, an elderly, nervous man who bought and sold Persian carpets, but was there because he was worried about his health and wished to consult the Embassy's medical adviser, Ahmed Dagdar.

Ten minutes after the arrival of the BBC team, Mustafa Karkouti, a Syrian journalist who was the European correspondent for *As-Afir*, the leading Beirut newspaper, arrived to interview the Embassy's cultural attaché, Dr Abul Fazi Ezzatti. Shown into Ezzatti's office, Room 13 on the third floor, he was offered a cup of coffee and proceeded with his interview while drinking it.

Another newsman present was Muhammad Farughi, a fifty-year-old British national born in India. He was the editor of *Impact International*, a Muslim magazine based in Finsbury Park, north London. Farughi had come to the Embassy for an interview with the chargé d'affaires, Dr Ali Afrouz, for an article about the Islamic revolution in Iran, and was at once escorted to the latter's office, at the front of the building, on the first floor, overlooking Princes Gate.

On arriving at the Embassy for his day of duty on behalf of the Diplomatic Protection Group, PC Lock took up his usual position outside, by the steps leading up to the front door. On this particular morning, however, which was particularly cold, he was offered a warming cup of tea by the sympathetic doorman, Abbas Fallahi. As it would not have been proper to have been seen drinking outside the building, the frozen policeman decided to take his tea in the small ante-room between the outside door and the heavy security doors leading to the entrance hall. So he was not present outside – and, even worse, the main door was ajar – when the six armed men from Baghdad arrived at the doorstep.

Number 105 Lexham Gardens, Earls Court Road, was rather more modest than the Iranian Embassy. An end-of-terrace Victorian house with five steps leading up to the front door, it had simulated tiles on the steps and yellow awnings above the window to give the façade the appearance of a colourful Continental hotel. Inside, it was less grand. The foyer was papered with gold-flecked wallpaper, the carpet was blood-red, and an office desk served as reception.

Flat 3, on the second floor, contained three bedrooms, two sitting-rooms, two bathrooms and a kitchen. The rooms had the tired, slightly tatty appearance of all bedsits and flats in the city, with unmatching furniture, fading wallpaper, and a combination of bare floorboards and loose, well-worn carpets.

At 9.40 a.m. on Wednesday, 30 April 1980, the six Iranians who had shared the flat with another, Sami Muhammad Ali, left it one by one and gathered in the foyer. They were all wearing anoraks to keep out the cold and to conceal the weapons they would soon collect.

The leader of the group, Oan-Ali, real name Salim Towfigh, had a frizzy Afro hairstyle, a bushy beard and sideburns. Twenty-seven years old, he was the only member of the group to speak English. His second in command was twenty-one-year-old Shakir Abdullah Fadhil, also known as Jasim or

Feisal, a so-called Ministry of Industry official who favoured jeans and cowboy boots and claimed to have once been tortured by SAVAK. The others were Fowzi Badavi Nejad, known as Ali, at nineteen the youngest and smallest member of the group; the short, heavily-built Shakir Sultan Said, or Shai, twenty-three and a former mechanic whose almost blond hair fell down over his ears; Makki Hounoun Ali, twenty-five, another Baghdad mechanic who now acted as the group's humble housekeeper; and a slim young man named Ali Abdullah, known as Nejad.

Though not as obviously dominant as Oan, Ali Abdullah was greatly respected by the others because his older brother Fa'ad was one of the most important leaders of the Democratic Revolutionary Front for the Liberation of Arabistan. Fa'ad Abdullah operated in exile in Iraq and broadcast regularly for the Arabic and Farsi sections of Radio Baghdad, exhorting the Iranians to rise up against the regime of the Ayatollahs.

Ali was a serious young man. More ebullient was Makki, who informed one of the other residents that the group was heading for France. In the foyer, Ali informed the Egyptian caretaker, Ahmed, that their nine bags, weighing a total of 203lb, would be collected by David Arafat, the property agent who had rented them the flat through his Tehar Service Agency in Earls Court Road. It would then be airfreighted back to Baghdad by him. After depositing the bags with Ahmed, the group left the building.

Makki waved goodbye to those watching through the glass doors of the foyer, then blew a handful of kisses and followed the others along the pavement.

For the next hour and a half, in the steel-grey morning light, the group moved from one safe house to another, collecting an arsenal of weapons that included two deadly Skorpion W263

Polish sub-machine-guns, three Browning self-loading pistols, one .38 Astra revolver, five Soviet-made RGD5 hand-grenades, and enough ammunition for a lengthy siege. By eleven-twenty the six men were assembled in Hyde Park, near the Albert Memorial, their weapons hidden under their coats, engaged in a last-minute discussion of their plans. Just before eleven-thirty, they left the park, crossed the road, and arrived outside 16 Princes Gate. The front door of the Embassy was ajar.

After covering their faces with the loose flap of their *keffias*, the traditional patterned Arab headdress, so that only their eyes and noses were visible, the men removed their weapons and stormed through the open front door of the Embassy, into the entrance hall. Hearing the commotion at the outer door, PC Lock darted out of the small ante-room and was practically bowled over by the terrorists rushing in. The deafening roar of automatic fire close to his ear was followed by the sound of smashing glass. A large slice of flying glass from the inner-door panel slashed PC Lock's cheek. Before he could remove his pistol, and as he was in the throes of sending an unfinished warning to Scotland Yard, one of the Arabs wrested the portable radio from him and another prodded his head with the barrel of a Maitraillette Vigneron M2 machine pistol. Putting up his hands, the policeman was prodded at gunpoint across the entrance hall, towards the door of reception.

Waiting there were Sim Harris, Chris Cramer, Ali Tabatabai and the highly strung Majtaba Mehrnavard, who all heard the roaring of the machine pistols, the smashing of glass and the thudding of bullets piercing the ceiling of the entrance hall. There followed frantic shouting in Arabic, then a voice bawling in Farsi: 'Don't move!' Understanding the words, Ali Tabatabai wanted to go out and see what was happening, but Cramer, an experienced newsman, stopped him with a curt 'No!' When he and the other BBC man, Sim Harris, turned to face the wall with their hands over their heads, Ali did the same.

A few seconds later PC Lock entered the room, his hands clutching his head, his face bloody. Following him were two women who also worked in the Embassy, and following them, prodding them along with semi-automatic weapons, were more terrorists with their faces veiled in *keffias*.

One of the veiled terrorists, speaking in English, warned the hostages that they would be killed if they moved, then he and the other terrorists led them at gunpoint across the entrance hall and up the stairs to the second floor.

On the third floor, the journalist Mustafa Karkouti was still deeply involved in his interview with Dr Ezzatti when he heard the machine-gun fire from below. Rushing from the office, both men saw other Embassy staff rushing past, heading down the stairs. Assuming that they were heading for a fire exit, Karkouti and Ezzatti followed them, but soon found themselves in another room that had no exit at all. There were about nine people in the room, including three or four women.

To protect all those gathered in the room, the door was locked from inside. Five minutes later, however, it was kicked open and one of the terrorists entered, looking like a bandit with his *keffia* around his face and a pistol in one hand and a grenade in the other. After firing an intimidating shot into the ceiling, he ordered everyone to place their hands on their head and face the wall. When they had done so, another man masked with a *keffia* entered the room and, with the help of the first man, guided the hostages at gunpoint down the stairs to the second floor, where other Embassy staff were standing with their hands on their heads, guarded by two other masked, armed terrorists.

Ron Morris, the caretaker, was still in his office on the fourth floor. Hearing the muffled sounds of gunfire, his first thought was that a student demonstration was under way, with the police firing blank cartridges. He ran down to the first floor, where he saw PC Lock and Abbas Fallahi with their hands on their heads, being guarded by an armed Arab. Morris instantly turned around and went back up to the second floor, where he passed an accountant, Mr Moheb. On asking the accountant what was happening, he received only a blank, dazed look. The caretaker hurried up to his office on the fourth floor, planning to phone the police, but just as he was dialling 999, he heard shouting and running feet on the stairs. Not wanting to be caught with the phone in his hand, he put it down and sat behind his desk until an armed terrorist entered. Speaking in English, the terrorist ordered him to leave the room, then prodded him at gunpoint down the stairs to Room 9A on the second floor, normally occupied by the Embassy's medical adviser, Dr Dadgar, but now filled with many hostages, all with their hands either against the wall or on their heads.

One of the gunmen searched the hostages. After frisking Morris, finding his spectacle case and throwing it to the floor, the gunman searched PC Lock, but in a manner so inept that he failed to find the policeman's holstered pistol.

While this search was going on, other members of the Embassy staff were managing to flee the building. Zari Afkhami, who was in charge of the medical section, had her office at the rear of the ground floor. Hearing the gunshots and shouting, she opened the door, stepped into the hall, and saw a gunman prodding PC Lock in the chest with a gun. Running back into her office and closing the door behind her, she alerted an elderly clerk who had a weak heart. Afkhami opened the window and climbed out, followed by the clerk. Catching sight of two workmen at the rear of the building, she asked them to call the police.

Another official escaped by boldly climbing out onto the first-floor balcony and making his way across a parapet to the Ethiopian Embassy next door.

One who attempted to escape, but failed, was the chargé d'affaires, Dr Afrouz, who was still being interviewed by the Muslim journalist Muhammad Farughi in his office on the first floor when the attack began. Hearing gunfire and shouting, both men went to the office door, where Farughi was instantly seized by a terrorist. Afrouz managed to make it back across to the rear of his office, where he clambered out through the window. Unfortunately, in his haste he fell, spraining his wrist and bruising his face badly. Hauled back in by the terrorists, he was prodded at gunpoint into a room where there were no other prisoners. There, one of the gunmen fired a shot into the ceiling, possibly to intimidate Afrouz. He then led the limping diplomat out of the room up the stairs to the second floor, where he was placed in Room 9A with the other prisoners.

Shocked by the appearance of the injured diplomat, and assuming that he had been beaten up by one of the terrorists, Ron Morris asked one of the terrorists for some water. He bathed Afrouz's face, then examined his jaw and confirmed that it was not broken. The chargé d'affaires, still shocked and in pain, fell asleep soon afterwards.

Informed of the attack on the Embassy, the police were already gathering outside. An officer entered the back garden, where he saw an armed Arab looking down at him from an upstairs window. Aiming his pistol at the terrorist, the police officer asked what the group wanted.

'If you take one more step you'll be shot,' the Arab replied in English.

By eleven-forty-five Scotland Yard knew that one of its men, PC Lock, was one of the hostages, that he belonged to the Diplomatic Protection Group, and that he had been armed. This last fact, combined with the information that gunshots had been heard, gave them further cause for concern.

By midday, the Embassy was surrounded by police cars and vans, ambulances, reporters, press photographers, and armed policemen wearing bulletproof vests. Other police officers were on the roof of the building, clearing spectators from the balconies of the adjoining buildings. More police were across the road, opposite the Embassy, clearing people out of the park and sealing off the area.

The siege had commenced.

1

The wind was howling over the Brecon Beacons as Staff-Sergeant Bill Harrison, huddled behind a rock for protection, surveyed the vast slopes of the Pen-y-Fan to find his four-man CRW (Counter Revolutionary Warfare) team. The men, he knew, would be feeling disgruntled because the tab he was making them undergo they had all endured before, during Initial Selection and Training, with all the horrors of Sickeners One and Two. The four men now climbing the steep, rocky slope were experienced SAS troopers who had fought in Aden, Oman or Belfast, and none required a second dose of the 'Long Drag' or 'Fan Dance' across this most inhospitable of mountain ranges – or, at least, would not have done so had they been asked to do it while carrying an Ingram 9mm sub-machine-gun and a 55lb bergen rucksack.

This time, however, there was a slight but diabolical turning of the screw: they were making the same arduous tab while wearing heavy CRW body armour, including ceramic plates front and back, and while breathing through a respirator mask fixed to a ballistic helmet. In short, they were being forced to endure hell on earth.

That was only part of it. Staff-Sergeant Harrison had not

only ordered them to climb to the summit of the mountain, but had then informed them that he would be giving them a thirty-minute head start, then following them to simulate pursuit by a real enemy. Thus, even as they would be fighting against exhaustion caused by the heavy body armour and murderous climb, as well as possible claustrophobia or disorientation caused by the cumbersome helmet and respirator mask, they would be compelled to concentrate on keeping out of Harrison's sub-machine-gun sight. This would place an even greater strain on them.

In fact, they had already failed in their task. Even though wearing his own body armour and head gear to ensure that his men would not feel he was asking them to do what he could not, the tough-as-nails staff-sergeant had taken another route up the mountain – to ensure that he was unseen by his men while they were always in his sight – and circled around them to take up this position above them, just below the rocky, wind-blown summit. The men would be broken up when they found him blocking their path, emulating an enemy sniper; but that, also, was part of this lesson in endurance.

Harrison had been a member of the 'Keeni Meeni' assassination squads in Aden in 1966, survived the incredible SAS hike up the mighty Jebel Dhofar in Oman in 1971 and, in 1976, spent days on end in freezing observation posts in the 'bandit country' of south Armagh, sweating it out, waiting to ambush IRA terrorists. For this reason he knew all about endurance and insisted that his men be prepared for it.

They had already lost this one, but they were still good men. Hiding behind his rock, one hand resting lightly on his PRC 319 radio, the other on his Ingram 9mm sub-machine-gun, which was loaded with live ammunition, Harrison watched the men advancing arduously up the slope and recalled how their work in Northern Ireland and led to their induction into the CRW.

All four men – Lance-Corporal Philip McArthur and Troopers Danny 'Baby Face' Porter, Alan Pyle and Ken Passmore – had been shipped in civilian clothing to Belfast immediately after being 'badged' in 1976. There they had specialized in intelligence gathering and ambush operations, working both in unmarked 'Q' cars in the streets and in OPs on the green hills of Armagh. By the end of their tour of duty in Northern Ireland, they were widely experienced in intelligence operations and therefore ideal material for special training in the 'killing house' in Hereford and subsequent transfer from their individual squadrons – B and D – to the Counter Revolutionary Warfare Wing.

Once in the CRW Wing, they were given more Close Quarters Battle (CQB) training in the 'killing house', then sent for various periods to train even more intensively with West Germany's CSG-9 border police and France's Groupement d'Intervention de la Gendarmerie Nationale (GIGN) para-military counter-terrorist units, the Bizondere Bystand Eenheid (BBE) counter-terrorist arm of the Royal Netherlands Marine Corps, Italy's Nucleo Operativo di Sicurezza (NOCS), Spain's Grupo Especial de Operaciones (GEO), and the US 1st Special Forces Operational Detachment, created specially for CRW operations.

The overseas postings had been designed to place a special emphasis on physical training and marksmanship. These included advanced, highly dangerous practice at indoor firing with live ammunition in other kinds of 'killing houses', such as mock-up aircraft, ships and public streets; abseiling and parachuting onto rooftops, parked aircraft and boats; hostage rescue in a variety of circumstances (which had the cross-over element of training in skiing, mountaineering and scuba diving); and the handling of CS gas canisters, and stun, fire and smoke grenades. Finally, they were taught how to deal with the hostages, physically and psychologically, once they had been rescued.

So, Harrison thought, those four hiking up the last yards to the summit of this mountain are going to be bitterly surprised at having lost – but they're still good men.

By now the four men were only about 20 yards below him, fifty from the summit, and obviously thinking they had managed to make it to the top without being caught. Wearing their all-black CRW overalls, respirator masks and NBC hoods, they looked frightening, but that did not deter Harrison. Smiling grimly, he raised his Ingram 9mm sub-machine-gun with its thirty-two-round magazine, pressed the extended stock into his shoulder, aimed at the marching men through his sight, then fired a short burst.

The noise broke the silence brutally. Harrison moved the gun steadily from left to right, tearing up soil and stones in an arc that curved mere inches in front of the marching men. Knowing that the bullets were real, they scuttled off the track in opposite directions, hurling themselves to the ground behind the shelter of rocks and screaming for Harrison to stop firing. Grinning more broadly, the staff-sergeant lowered his Ingram, put the safety-catch back on, then used the PRC 319 radio to call the leader of the four-man team, Lance-Corporal Philip McArthur.

'You dumb bastards. You're all dead meat,' the message said.

Lying behind the rocks lower down the windswept slope, the four men received the message with incredulity, then, almost

16

instinctively, turned their surprised gaze to the exploded soil that had cut an arc just a short distance in front of where they had been walking, practically up to their feet.

'I don't believe it!' Trooper Alan Pyle exclaimed, removing his respirator mask from his face as the others did the same, all relieved to be breathing pure, freezing air. 'That daft bastard was using live ammo and nearly shot our fucking toes off.'

'He's too good for that,' Trooper Danny 'Baby Face' Porter said. 'If he'd wanted to shoot your toes off, you can be sure he'd have done it.'

'Just like you, eh?' said the third trooper, Ken Passmore, grinning admiringly. 'A real crack shot.'

'Yeah,' Baby Face replied with modest pride. 'I suppose you could say that.'

'All right, all right,' snapped Lance-Corporal Phil McArthur. 'Stop the backslapping. We've nothing to be proud of. After all, we *were* as good as dead. Now let's pick up our gear and go and face the great man.'

Breathing more easily without the masks, but crushed by being 'killed' by Harrison, the men picked up their weapons and other kit and advanced up the hill until they reached the staff-sergeant. Squatting behind the rock with a big grin on his face, Harrison was strapping the PRC 319 to his shoulders and picking up his Ingram.

'Nice try, men,' he said, 'but if this had been a real operation you'd all be belly up by now. Are you SAS men or not?'

'Fucking 'ell, Sarge,' Phil McArthur protested as he glanced back down the mountain at the broad sweep of the Brecon Beacons far below. 'We could hardly breathe in these bloody masks. And that hike was a killer.'

'Piece of piss,' Harrison replied. 'I got this far without taking a deep breath. I think you need some more exercise.'

The men stared warily at him. All of them were breathing heavily and still bathed in sweat, even though the wind was howling across the mountain, slapping icily at them.

'No more exercise, please,' Ken Passmore said, already drained. 'I can't move another inch.'

Harrison grinned with sly malice. 'What were your instructions, Trooper?'

'To get to the summit of the mountain,' Ken replied, 'without being shot or captured by you.'

'Which you were.'

'Right.'

'Which doesn't mean it's over, you daft prat. You've still got to get to the summit, so get up and go, all of you.'

In disbelief the breathless men glanced up to the summit, which was 50 yards higher up, though the distance seemed far greater and the steepness of the climb was horrendous.

'Jesus, Sarge,' Alan complained. 'After the climb we've just made, that last leg is going to be impossible.'

'Right,' Ken said. 'That slope is a killer.'

'Either you make that climb,' Harrison told them, 'or I have you RTU'd and standing by dusk on Platform 4, Hereford Station, outward bound. Get the message?'

'Yes, Sarge.'

'Come on,' Baby Face shouted. 'Let's get up and go.'

Though still trying to get their breath back, the weary men covered their heads and faces again with the respirator masks and ballistic helmets, humped their bergens onto their backs, picked up their Ingrams and reluctantly began the steep climb to the summit.

Within a few yards they were already gasping for breath, their feet slipping on smooth rocks, bodies tensed against the wind, the sweat soon dripping from their foreheads into their eyes. Twenty yards on, where the wind was even more fierce, the slope rose at an angle so steep it was almost vertical. Holding their sub-machine-guns in one hand and clinging to rocks with the other, they laboriously hauled themselves up until, about 20 yards from the summit, all of them except Baby Face decided to give in. Falling behind, they just leaned against high rocks, fighting to regain their breath, about to call it a day.

Harrison's Ingram roared into life as he fired a short burst in an arc that tore up earth and pieces of splintered rock mere inches from the feet of the men who had given up. Shocked, they lurched away from the spitting soil and scrambled with a strength they had felt had been drained out of them up the last, cruel section of the slope. Each time they fell back, another roar from the Ingram, ripping up the soil and rocks just behind the men, forced them to move hastily higher, finally following Baby Face off the sheer slope and onto the more even summit.

When the last of them had clambered onto the highest point, gasping but still surprised at their hitherto untapped stamina, Harrison followed them up and told them to remove the masks and breathe proper air. When the men had done so, they were able to look down on the fabulous panorama of the Brecon Beacons, spread out all around them, wreathed in mist, streaked with sunshine, thousands of feet below. Lying there, now completely exhausted, they gulped the fresh, freezing air, grateful that they would at last be able to take a good break.

Just as they were about to have a brew-up, a message came through on the radio. Harrison listened intently, then said: 'Got it, boss. Over and out.' Replacing the microphone on its hook, he turned to his weary men. 'Sorry, lads, no brew-up yet. We've got to return straightaway. The Iranian Embassy in London has been seized and we're being put on stand-by. This isn't a mock exercise. It's the real thing. So pack your kit and let's hike back to the RV.'

Recharged by the prospect of real action, the men hurriedly packed up and began the hazardous descent.

2

By three p.m. on the first day, in a basement office in Whitehall a top-level crisis management team known as COBR, representing the Cabinet Office Briefing Room, was having a tense discussion about the raid on the Iranian Embassy. Presiding over the meeting was a man of some eminence, addressed as the 'Secretary', Junior Defence and Foreign Affairs ministers, representatives of MI5 and the Metropolitan Police, including the Police Commissioner, and the overall commander of the SAS CBQ team, addressed as the 'Controller', though in fact he was much more than that when it came to issues involving international politics and the defence of the realm.

'The function of this meeting,' the surprisingly genial and unruffled Secretary said, 'is to lay down guidelines for the police and, if necessary, the Army. First, however, the Commissioner of the Metropolitan Police will fill us in on the general situation.'

The Commissioner cleared his throat and sized up his audience before speaking. 'The Embassy is being held by a six-man team of Iranians who were trained in Iraq, issued with Iraqi passports, and supplied with weapons brought in by diplomatic bag from Baghdad. We now know that they all visited the British Embassy in Baghdad last February to pick up individual visas to visit the UK. When asked how they would live in the UK, they each produced the same amount of cash: £275. In each case the purpose of the visit was recorded as being for medical treatment. Once in London, they were placed under the command of an Iraqi army officer, Sami Muhammad Ali, who flew home the day the siege began.'

'Who's leading them now?' the Secretary asked.

The Commissioner showed them a picture of a well-built Arab with frizzy hair, a bushy beard and long sideburns. 'The ringleader, Oan-Ali,' he said. 'Real name Salim Towfigh. Twenty-seven years old. Records show that he comes from Al Muhammara in the Khuzistan province of Iran, just across the Shatt-al-Arab river border with Iraq. Studied languages and law at Tehran University, where he became politically active and eventually militant. Fluent in four languages: Farsi, Arabic, German and English. He's believed to be one of those who took part in the riots that occurred there on 29 May last year, when 220 men and women in the crowd were reported killed and approximately 600 wounded. Certainly he was imprisoned and tortured by SAVAK, which only made him more militant. On 31 March this year he turned up with four other Arabs in Earls Court Road, where they took two flats at 20 Nevern Place. One of the flats was on the second floor, the other in the basement. Only three of the men signed the register: Oan-Ali, Makki Hounoun Ali, and Shakir Abdullah Fadhil. The caretaker was an Iraqi student studying computer engineering. He says he didn't examine their passports thoroughly, though he noted that they were issued in Iraq. The men told him they had just flown in from Baghdad. Apart from that, the caretaker learnt little about them. They claimed to have met each other by chance on the plane to

London. One said he was a farmer, the other a student, the third a mechanic. The group is particularly remembered by the caretaker and other members of the household because, though Muslims, they came in late at night, invariably drunk and often with local prostitutes. Eventually, when they became embroiled in an argument over prices with one of the ladies in the basement flat, the caretaker, a devout Muslim, threw them out of the house.'

'Sounds like they weren't particularly sophisticated,' the Secretary said. 'Muslims seduced instantly by Western ways: alcohol and sex. Certainly not very disciplined.'

'That's worth bearing in mind,' the Controller said. 'A lack of discipline in a siege situation could go either way: either helping us to succeed or leading to mayhem and slaughter.'

Deliberately pausing to let the Controller's words sink in, the Commissioner then continued reading from his notes: 'After being thrown out of the house in Nevern Place, the terrorists dropped into the Tehar Service Agency, an accommodation agency run by a Jordanian named David Arafat and special-izing in Arab clients with plenty of money and often dubious intentions. Arafat rarely asked questions of his clients, but claims that Oan-Ali told him he had left his previous accom-modation because his group had been joined by two other friends and they needed larger accommodation. Subsequently, Arafat fixed them up with Flat 3, 105 Lexham Gardens, just a few hundred yards north of his Earls Court Road office.'

'And *were* there more men at this point?' the Controller asked.

'No,' the Commissioner replied. 'It was the same five who had been in Nevern Place who took over the flat in Lexham Gardens. However, the flat has three bedrooms, two sitting-rooms, two bathrooms and a kitchen, and according to the

Egyptian caretaker, the five-man group grew to seven over the next few days. After that, there were times when as many as a dozen men would be there at the same time.'

'Do we know who the others were?' the Controller asked.

'No. We *do* know, however, that some of the others in his group are former members of the Democratic Revolutionary Front for the Liberation of Arabistan and that one of them, Fa'ad, broadcasts for the Arabic and Farsi sections of Radio Baghdad, exhorting the people of Iran to rise up against the regime of the Ayatollahs.'

As the Controller nodded and wrote in his notebook, the Commissioner concentrated once more on the file opened on the table before him. 'Intelligence has reason to believe that though Oan-Ali led the raid, he didn't actually plan it himself. One of those who moved into 105 Lexham Gardens was Sami Muhammad Ali, an Iraqi army officer described in his passport as an official of the Iraqi Ministry of Industry. Other meetings which Ali was known to have attended took place at 55 and 24 Queens Gate, the latter only two doors up from the office of the Iraqi military attaché.'

'How ironic!' the Secretary purred, smiling like a Cheshire cat.

'Finally,' the Commissioner continued reading, 'on 29 April, the day before the seizure of the Embassy, it was Oan-Ali who visited David Arafat, the property agent, to tell him that his friends were leaving Lexham Gardens – supposedly going to Bristol for a week, then returning to Iraq. He asked Arafat to crate their baggage and air-freight it back to Baghdad. The address he gave was a post-box number. By the following morning, when the rest of the group seized the Embassy, Oan-Ali had disappeared.'

'How many hostages?' the Controller asked.

'Twenty-two in all. Fifteen Iranians, the British caretaker, one Diplomatic Protection Group police constable, and five visitors, four of whom are journalists. The DPG constable, PC Lock, had a pistol concealed on his person and may still possess it.'

'That could be helpful,' the Secretary said with a hopeful smile.

'Or dangerous,' the Controller reminded him, then turned back to the Commissioner. 'Do we know more about the hostages?'

'One is Mustafa Karkouti, the European correspondent for *As-Afir*, the leading Beirut newspaper. Thirty-seven years old, he's Syrian by birth, but educated in Damascus and Beirut. He was known to be pursuing the story of the hostages held by Iranian students at the American Embassy in Tehran. We also know that a month ago he attended an Islamic conference in London, to hear a speech by the Iranian Embassy's cultural attaché, Dr Abul Fazi Ezzatti. He then fixed up a meeting with Dr Ezzatti at the Embassy for Wednesday, 30 April, at eleven a.m. He was there when the terrorists seized the building.'

'Any use to us?' the Secretary asked.

'Could be. He speaks fluent English and Arabic, as well as a fair bit of Farsi.'

'That could come in handy.'

'Exactly. Also useful is the fact that Karkouti works out of Fleet Street and lives with his wife and child in Ealing. He therefore knows the English mentality, as well as the Iranian, which could be helpful to my negotiators.'

'Who else?'

'Ron Morris, a forty-seven-year-old Englishman, born in Battersea, London. Son of the station-master at Waterloo. Left school at fourteen, spent six months in a factory in Battersea, then obtained a job as an office boy for the Iranian Embassy. That was in 1947 and, apart from his two years' National Service, he's worked for the Iranians ever since – first as an office boy, then as a chauffeur, and finally as caretaker and general maintenance man. In 1970, when he'd been with them for twenty-five years, he was given a long-service bonus of a ten-day trip to Iran.'

'Is he political?'

'No, Mr Secretary. He's a regular, down-to-earth type, not easily ruffled. Reportedly, he views himself as being above politics. Lives with an Italian wife and a cat in a basement flat in Chester Street, Belgravia. Collects replica guns. His work for the Iranians is certainly not political.'

'So he could be useful.'

'Yes and no. As the maintenance man, he knows every nook and cranny in the building. That knowledge could encourage him to try to escape.'

'And the others?'

'The Diplomatic Protection Group's Police Constable Trevor Lock. Known as a good man. He had a standard police-issue .38 Smith and Wesson revolver holstered on the thigh and so far there's no report that the terrorists have found it. According to a recent report, however, Lock was slightly hurt and is bleeding from the face.'

'Have the hostages made contact yet?'

'Yes, Mr Secretary. Ninety minutes after the seizure of the Embassy, the terrorists asked for a woman doctor to be sent in. At first we assumed this was for PC Lock, but in fact it was for the Embassy Press Officer, Mrs Frieda Mozafarian, who's had a series of fainting fits combined with muscular spasms. Lock is apparently OK – just a little bruised and bloody.'

'So how do we handle this?' the Secretary asked.

The Commissioner coughed into his fist. 'First, the police will negotiate with the terrorists. Undoubtedly the terrorists will want media coverage of their demands, so we'll use this as a bargaining chip. As their demands won't be directed at the British Government, but at the Iranians, we can afford to cede this to them.'

He paused, waiting for their reaction.

'Go on,' the Secretary said, clasping his hands under his chin and looking disingenuously benign.

'Having met them halfway with media exposure for their demands,' the Commissioner continued, 'we try to talk them out, letting the affair stretch on for as long as necessary. During that period, we'll attempt to soften them up with food, medical attention, communications, more access to the media, and the involvement of their own ambassadors and those of other friendly Middle Eastern states. We'll also ask for the release of certain hostages, particularly those ill or wounded. This will not only reduce the number of hostages to be dealt with, but encourage the terrorists to feel that they're contributing to a real, on-going dialogue. In fact, what we'll be doing is buying enough time for the police and MI5 to plant miniature listening devices inside the building and also scan it with parabolic directional microphones and thermal imagers. Between these, they should at least show us just where the hostages are being held.'

'And what happens when the terrorists' patience runs out?'

'Should negotiations fail and, particularly, if the terrorists kill a hostage, or hostages, clearance will be given for the SAS to attack the building.'

The Home Secretary turned his attention to the Controller, who looked handsome in his beret with winged-dagger badge. 'Are you prepared for this?'

'Yes, sir. The operation will be codenamed "Pagoda". We'll use the entire counter-terrorist squadron: a command group of four officers plus a fully equipped support team consisting of one officer and twenty-five other ranks, ready to move at thirty minutes' notice. A second team, replicating the first, will remain on a three-hour stand-by until the first team has left the base. A third team, if required, can be composed from experienced SAS soldiers. The close-quarters support teams are backed up by sniper groups who will pick off targets from outside the Embassy and specially trained medical teams to rescue and resuscitate the hostages.'

'You are, of course, aware of the importance of police primacy in this matter?'

The Controller nodded. 'Yes, Mr Secretary. Coincidentally, we've just been preparing for a joint exercise with the Northumbria Police Force, so the men and equipment are all in place at Hereford. That's only 150 miles, or less than three hours' drive, away. We're ready to roll, sir.'

'Excellent.' The Secretary turned to the Metropolitan Police Commissioner. 'Do you have any problems with this scenario?'

'No,' the Commissioner replied. 'My views today are those of Sir Robert Mark regarding the Spaghetti House siege of 1975. Those terrorists will either come out to enter a prison cell or end up in a mortuary. They'll have no other option.'

Some of the men smiled. The Home Secretary, looking satisfied, spread his hands out on the table. 'To summarize, gentlemen . . . There will be no surrender to the terrorists. No safe conduct for the terrorists out of the country. Either this affair ends peacefully, with the surrender of the terrorists, or the SAS go in and bring them out, dead or alive. Agreed?'

The men of COBR were in total agreement.

3

As the team on the Pen-y-Fan were contending with the arduous return hike to the four-ton Bedford lorry that would take them back to Bradbury Lines, the SAS base in Hereford, another team, consisting of Staff-Sergeant 'Jock' Thompson, Corporal George 'GG' Gerrard, Lance-Corporal Dan 'Danny Boy' Reynolds and Trooper Robert 'Bobs-boy' Quayle were dressing up in heavy CRW Bristol body armour with high-velocity ceramic plates, S6 respirator masks to protect them from CS gas, black ballistic helmets and skin-tight aviator's gloves in the 'spider', their eight-legged dormitory area, in the same base in Hereford. They did not take too much pleasure in doing so.

'I hate this fucking gear,' Corporal 'GG' Gerrard complained, slipping on his black flying gloves. 'I feel like a bloody deep-sea diver, but I'm walking on dry land.'

'I agree,' Lance-Corporal 'Danny Boy' Reynolds said, adjusting the ballistic helmet on his head and reluctantly picking up his respirator. 'This shit makes me feel seasick.'

'I *hate* the sea,' the relatively new man, Trooper 'Bobs-boy' Quayle, said grimly, 'so these suits give me nightmares.'

'Excuse me?' Staff-Sergeant 'Jock' Thompson asked.

'What, Sarge?' Bobs-boy replied.

'Did I hear you say that suit gives you nightmares?'

'That's right, Sarge, you heard me right.'

'So what the fuck are you doing in this CT team?' Thompson asked.

Bobs-boy shrugged. 'I'm pretty good with the Ingram,' he explained, 'close quarters battle.'

'But you suffer from nightmares.'

The trooper started to look uncomfortable. 'Well . . . I didn't mean it *literally*. I just meant . . .'

Danny Boy laughed. 'Literally? What kind of word is that? Is that some kind of new SAS jargon?'

'He's an intellectual,' GG explained.

'Who gets nightmares,' Danny Boy added.

'A nightmare-sufferer and an intellectual prat to boot,' Jock clarified. 'And we've got him on *our* team!'

'I didn't mean . . .' Bobs-boy began.

'Then you shouldn't have said it,' the staff-sergeant interjected. 'If you get nightmares over CRW gear, we don't want you around here, kid.'

'Dreams,' Bobs-boy said quickly. 'I meant *dreams*. Really nice ones as well, Sarge. Not nightmares at all. I dream a lot about scuba diving and things like that, so this gear suits me nicely, thanks.'

'You can see how he got badged,' GG told the others with a wink. 'It's his talent for knowing which way the winds blows and always saying the right thing.'

'The only sound that pleases me is his silence,' Jock said, 'and I'd like that right now. Put those respirators on your ugly mugs and let's get to the killing house.'

'Yes, boss,' they all chimed, then covered their faces with the respirator masks. Though this kept them from talking casually, they could still communicate, albeit with eerie distortion, through their Davies Communications CT100E headset and microphone. However, once the respirators were attached to the black ballistic helmets, they looked like goggle-eyed deep-sea monsters with enormously bulky, black-and-brown, heavily armoured bodies – inhuman and frightening.

'Can you all hear me?' Jock asked, checking his communications system.

'Check, Corporal Gerrard.'

'Check, Lance-Corporal Reynolds.'

'Check, Trooper Quayle.'

All the men gave the thumbs-up sign as they responded. When the last of them – Bobs-boy – stuck his thumb up, Jock did the same, then used a hand signal to indicate that they should follow him out of the spider.

After cocking the action of their weapons, they introduced live rounds to the chamber, applied the safety-catch, then proceeded to the first of six different 'killing rooms' in the CQB House for a long day's practice. Here they fired 'double taps' from the Browning 9mm High Power handgun, known as the '9-milly', and short bursts from their Ingram 9mm sub-machine-guns, at various pop-up 'figure eleven' targets. They were also armed with real Brocks Pyrotechnics MX5 stun grenades.

The 'killing house' had been constructed to train SAS troopers in the skills required to shoot assassins or kidnappers in the close confines of a building without hitting the hostage. As he led his men into the building, Jock felt a definite underlying resentment about what he was doing.

The Regiment's first real experience in urban terrorism had been in Palestine, where SAS veteran Major Roy Farran had conceived the idea of having men infiltrate the urban population by dressing up as natives and then assassinating known enemies at close quarters, usually with a couple of shots from a handgun. Though Jock had never worked with Farran, he had been a very young man in Aden in 1964 when Farran's basic theories had been used as the basis for the highly dangerous work of the Keeni Meeni squads operating in the souks and bazaars. There, teams of men, including Jock, all specially trained in CQB and disguised as Arabs, had mingled with the locals to gun down known Yemeni guerrillas.

Loving his work, dangerous though it had been, Jock had been shocked by the extent of his boredom when, back in Britain, he had been RTU'd to his original unit, the 2nd Battalion, Scots Guards, for a long bout of post-Suez inactivity. Though he subsequently married and had children – Tom, Susan, then Ralph, now all in their teens – he had never managed completely to settle down into the routine of peacetime army life.

For that reason he had applied for a transfer to the SAS, endured the horrors of Initial Selection and Training, followed by Continuation Training and parachute jumping in Borneo. Badged, he had fought with the Regiment in Oman in the early 1970s. Unfortunately, he returned from Oman to more years of relative boredom until 1976, when he was posted to Northern Ireland, where, in Belfast and south Armagh, he learnt just about all there was to know about close-quarters counter-terrorist warfare.

Posted back from Northern Ireland, Jock was again suffering the blues of boredom when, luckily for him, the Commanding Officer of 22 SAS decided to keep his CQB specialists busy by having them train bodyguards for overseas heads of state supportive of British interests. One of those chosen for this dangerous, though oddly glamorous, task was Jock, who, bored with his perfectly good marriage, was delighted to be able to travel the world with diplomatic immunity and a Browning 9mm High Power handgun hidden in the cross-draw position under his well-cut grey suit.

During those years, when most routine close protection of UK diplomats in political hotspots was handled by the Royal Military Police, the SAS were still being called in when the situation was particularly dangerous. For this reason, the need for men specially trained in close-quarters work led to the formation of the Counter Revolutionary Warfare Wing.

In Munich in September 1972, the Palestinian terrorist group Black September took over an Olympic Games village dormitory and held Israeli athletes hostage, leading to a bloody battle with West German security forces in which all the hostages, five terrorists and one police officer were killed. The shocked West German and French governments responded by forming their own anti-terrorist squads. In Britain, this led to the formation of a special SAS Counter-Terrorist (CT) team that would always be available at short notice to deal with hijacks and sieges anywhere in the United Kingdom. Those men, like their predecessors in Aden and in the CRW, had been trained in the 'killing house'. Jock Thompson was one of them.

The CQB House is dubbed the 'killing house' for two good reasons. The first is that its purpose is to train men to kill at close quarters. The second is that real ammunition is used and that at least one SAS man has been killed accidentally while training with it.

Jock was mindful of this chilling fact as he led his four-man CT team into the building and along the first corridor, toward rooms specially constructed to simulate most of the situations an SAS man would encounter during a real hostage-rescue operation. The men had already been trained to enter captured buildings by a variety of means, including abseiling with ropes from the roof, sometimes firing a Browning 9mm High Power handgun with one hand as they clung to the rope with the other. This particular exercise, however, was to make them particularly skilled at distinguishing instantly between terrorist and hostage. It was done with the aid of pictures on the walls and dummies that were moved from place to place, or that popped out suddenly from behind artificial walls or up from the lower frame of windows.

This began happening as Jock and his men moved along the first corridor. Dummy figures bearing painted weapons popped out from behind opening doors or window frames to be peppered by a fusillade of bullets from the real weapons of the training team. Once the targets had looked like Russians; now they were men in anoraks and balaclava helmets.

The major accomplishment lay not in hitting the 'terrorists' but in *not* hitting a 'hostage' instead. This proved particularly difficult when they had less than a second to distinguish between a dummy that was armed and one that was not. To hit the latter too many times was to invite a humiliating rejection by the SAS and the ignominy of being RTU'd.

The exercise could have been mistaken for a childish game, except for one thing – like the weapons, the bullets were real.

Completing a successful advance along the first couple of corridors, Jock's team then had to burst into various rooms, selected from drawings of the reconstructed killing house, shown to them during their briefing.

The CT team is divided into two specialist groups: the assault group, who enter the building, and the 'perimeter containment' group, consisting of snipers who provide a cordon sanitaire around the scene. In this instance, Jock and his men were acting as an assault group. This meant that they had to burst into a room in pairs and instantly fire two pistol rounds or short, controlled bursts of automatic fire – the famed SAS 'double tap' – into each terrorist, aiming for the head, without causing injury to either fellow team members or the hostages.

Reaching their selected rooms, the four-man team divided into two pairs, each with its own room to clear. Leading Red Team, with Danny Boy as his back-up, Jock blasted the metal lock off with a burst from his Remington 870 pump-action shotgun, dropped to one knee as the lock blew apart, with pieces of wood and metal flying out in all directions, then cocked the Browning pistol in his free hand and bawled for Danny Boy to go in.

The lance-corporal burst in ahead of Thompson, hurling an instantaneous safety electric fuse before him as he went. The thunderous flash of the ISFE exploded around both men as they rushed in and made their choice between a number of targets – the terrorists standing, the hostages sitting in chairs. They took out the former without hitting the latter, delivering accurate double taps to the head in each case.

Each man had his own preselected arc of fire, which prevented him hitting one of his own men. In this instance, the two men could easily have done this when they burst from a 'rescued' room back into the corridor to come face to face with either another dummy or with the other team, Corporal 'GG' Gerrard and Trooper Robert Quayle. Likewise, when Blue Team burst out of their own 'rescued' room, they often did so just as a dummy popped out from behind a swinging door, or up from behind a window frame, very close to them. The chilling possibility of an 'own goal' was always present.

Even so, while the men had found this form of training exciting, or frightening, in the early days, by now it had become too familiar to present any novelty. To make their frustration more acute, once the figures had been 'stitched' with bullets, or the room 'cleared' of terrorists, the men then had to paste paper patches over the holes in the figures, using a paste-brush and brown paper, in order that the targets could be used again by those following them. Because they had to do this mundane task themselves – even though they were firing real weapons, exploding ISFE, and hurling stun grenades – they became increasingly bored as they made their way through the various rooms of the killing house.

Their irritation was made all the worse by the fact that a day of such training led not only to sweaty exhaustion, but to raging headaches from the acrid pall of smoke and lead fumes which filled the killing house. So, when finally they had completed their 'rescue' and could stumble out into the fresh air, they were immensely relieved.

'I'll tell you something,' Danny Boy said later, as they were showering in the ablutions of the spider. 'If I don't get killed accidentally by one of you bastards during those exercises, I'll be killed by the fucking boredom of doing them over and over again.'

'They don't bore *me*,' Bobs-boy said. 'I just hate the CRW suits and body armour and helmet and mask. I feel buried alive in them.'

'You feel buried alive because you're like the walking dead,' GG taunted him. 'You're as limp as your dick, kid.'

'Nightmares!' Danny Boy exclaimed.

'Dreams,' Bobs-boy corrected him.

'All I know,' GG said, 'is that we haven't done a real job since Northern Ireland and we've now had four years of bullshit. One more run through that bloody killing house and I'm all set for the knacker's yard.'

'Or Ward 11 of the British Army Psychiatric Unit,' Danny Boy said, 'like Sergeant "Ten Pints and a Knuckle Sandwich" Inman.'

'Sergeant Inman was in a psychiatric ward?' the relatively new Bobs-boy asked incredulously.

'Correct,' GG replied. 'Oman, Belfast, Hong Kong and then straight into the horrors of Ward 11, where – I have it on the best authority – he made the insane look sane.'

'But Sergeant Inman's supposed to be one of the best soldiers in the Regiment,' Bobs-boy said, looking even more puzzled.

'He is,' Danny Boy replied. 'He just happens to have a couple of little problems that have to be sorted out.'

'And they let him stay on with the Regiment?' Bobs-boy asked, stupefied.

'Right,' GG said. 'He likes a pint – or twenty – followed up by a dust-up. He's only unhappy when he's not fighting.'

'Not giving knuckle sandwiches, you understand,' Danny Boy added. 'By fighting, we mean doing our job, which isn't scrapping in pubs.'

'And the fact that we haven't done that since Northern Ireland,' GG said, 'which is all of four years ago, is what's driving us – and Sergeant Inman – mad.'

'He's with the Commandos at the moment,' Bobs-boy said. 'That should keep him happy.'

'It doesn't keep *me* happy,' Danny Boy said. 'One more run around that fucking killing house and I'm going to kill myself.'

'Hey, you lot!' Jock bellowed as he entered the ablutions and looked in disgust at the naked men under the steaming showers.

'The Head Shed,' the staff-sergeant told them, referring to their Commanding Officer, 'has just received a message

37

from the Kremlin – the intelligence section at Regimental HQ, in case you new boys don't remember. They told him, through the Metropolitan Police, that a group of armed terrorists has taken over the Iranian Embassy. The Bedfords will get us there in three hours, so get your bare arses out of those showers and cover them up and get ready. We leave in one hour.'

Dripping wet and naked as the day they were born, the three men cheered and clapped at the news.

4

In the Royal Marines Commando Training Centre in Devon, SAS Sergeant Inman, formerly with the Royal Engineers, now thirty-eight years of age, was frog-marched between two NCO Military Policemen into an office where the Commanding Officer of the base, Lieutenant-Colonel William Fairworth, was seated behind his desk, studying the notes before him and sardonically raising his eyebrows at the SAS sergeant sitting in a wooden chair beside him. When Sergeant Inman had snapped to attention between the two MPs and saluted the CO, the latter stared steadily at him before saying: 'At ease, Sergeant.'

Inman stood at ease. Lieutenant-Colonel Fairworth glanced at the notes, then looked up and said: 'Drunk and disorderly again, Sergeant. This is no laughing matter.'

'Beg to differ, sir, but the other man threw the first punch, so I'd no choice in the matter.'

'You're being disingenuous, Sergeant. What matters is not who threw the first punch, but who started the argument.'

'He insulted the Regiment, boss.'

'Sir!' SAS Sergeant Shannon snapped. 'You are talking to the Commando CO – not the SAS. We don't use the word "boss" here.'

'Sorry, Sergeant. Keep forgetting.'

'You forget a bit too much for my liking,' Fairworth said, glancing down at the report again. 'Such as respect for the traditions of other regiments, which is why you get into trouble in pubs.'

'I can't help myself, sir.'

That much was true. Sergeant Inman had been on the sniper course for only a fortnight, but during that time he had been brought back by the MPs three or four times, either for plain drunkenness or for fighting in some pub or other. In fact, he was bored out of his mind and had had enough of the Commandos. He wanted to go back to Hereford with the men and routines he knew and loved.

'You have an interesting track record, Sergeant Inman. Royal Engineers, then with the SAS in Oman, Belfast and Hong Kong, always with commendable results. Unfortunately, you appear to be unable to get anything right once you're in a non-fighting environment. This has led to psychiatric problems that were treated – supposedly successfully.'

Sergeant Inman winced, having hoped that the Royal Marine Commando CO would not have been informed of his little experience in the psychiatric unit of the British Army.

Well, fuck it, he thought. He should never have been sent there in the first place. Or, perhaps he should have been, since the psychiatrists were even madder than the patients, though with much less reason.

He had his reasons, after all. He had been suffering from the exhaustion of a long run of ugly business: first the assault on the Jebel Massif in Oman, then Operation Jaguar, also in Oman, then the now legendary Battle of Mirbat, which even to this day gave him bad dreams and soaked his sheets in sweat.

Some good men had died there. Their deaths had been gruesome. To make matters worse, the survivors had been returned to a Britain that did not know they existed – neither them nor the battle.

Of course, that was the SAS way. Anonymity was everything. Nevertheless, Inman had found it pretty odd to have fought such a mighty battle, such a bloody affair, only to return home to an official silence that had made him feel worthless.

Exhaustion – certainly. But also something much more than that: the emptiness of not being recognized, of being cast aside, combined with the terminal boredom of having nothing to do in a non-combatant environment.

True enough, Inman was already feeling depleted when they sent him to Northern Ireland and the Q cars and covert observation. A right nasty job, that one. By the time he returned again to the SAS Sports and Social Club in Redhill, Hereford, he had killed too many in CQB and was feeling sick to his soul.

Of course by that time, also, he needed it and could not live without it . . . Which is why he had taken up drinking and getting into the odd fight. This, in its turn, was why he had ended up in Ward 11 with all those barmy shrinks.

So how did he deal with this matter when facing a Royal Marines Commando CO who did not know about his traumas and probably resented the SAS anyway?

Be bold. Who dares wins.

'Not supposedly, sir,' Inman replied boldly. 'The treatment was one hundred per cent successful.'

'That may be the case, but I have to warn you, Sergeant, that your habit of drunken fights, table-smashing and insubordination is not being applauded. The fact that you're a particularly good soldier in battle conditions is not going to save you if, as I think is happening, you start being seen as an over-the-hill, alcoholic troublemaker.'

'I'm not alcoholic, sir,' Inman said, as bold as brass. 'I only drink too much when I'm not fighting – overseas with the Regiment, that is.'

'Is that supposed to be a joke?' Sergeant Shannon asked.

'No, Sarge. The plain, unvarnished truth. No amount of training or retraining will keep me satisfied. I need a real operation.'

Though both men were sergeants, Shannon was in this case acting as second in command to the CO.

'We can't create operations just for you, Sergeant. You're thirty-eight and experienced enough to know that at this stage of your career most of your time will be taken up with training, retraining and guard duties. You should count yourself lucky that, given your age, not to mention your psychiatric history, you were still chosen for this Commando sniper course rather than cross-graining the bukits for the nth time on the Pen-y-Fan.'

Why the fuck don't you just stop yapping, Inman thought, and send me back to the Regiment, where I belong? I won't beat up any of your bloody Commandos, then. I'll be a good little boy.

'I do appreciate that, sir, but I just can't get my act together here. I feel all out of sorts.'

'You've always felt out of sorts,' Shannon snorted. 'That's why you had psychiatric treatment. You can't adjust to anything but war. I'd call that unhealthy.'

'Quite so,' Lieutenant-Colonel Fairworth said, glancing again at the report lying open on his desk. 'The evidence certainly indicates that you're totally unsuitable to a peacetime Army, whether it be in the Royal Engineers, the SAS or here. I'm thinking of recommending that you be RTU'd back to the

Royal Engineers and there put up for summary discharge from the service.'

'Please don't do that, sir.' Now Inman was seriously worried that he might have overstepped the mark. This was a Commando officer – not a member of the SAS. In the latter Regiment, a tolerance for individual eccentricities was customary and Inman had survived many an episode for that very reason. Though aware of his own explosive tensions, his tendency to become rapidly bored, and his irresistible need to release his frustrations with bouts of heavy drinking and fighting, he was unable to control these impulses and knew that they would get him into serious trouble sooner or later. That time might have come. The very thought of being thrown out of the Regiment filled him with panic. 'I promise to control myself in the future and concentrate on the training,' he mumbled.

'I'll personally guarantee that he does that,' Shannon said. Having served with Inman in Oman and Belfast, he admired him as a soldier and felt a great deal of loyalty towards him. He and Inman had been through a lot together and that counted for something. Also, regardless of his many faults, Inman was a damned good soldier who deserved to stay with the Regiment. 'I'll do it if I have to work him into the ground. He won't get time to make a fool of himself again. Put him under my wing, sir.'

Fairworth studied Inman's report, shook his head wearily, then gently closed the manila folder. Turning to Shannon, he said: 'That's an admirable offer, Sergeant, but I'm afraid I have to reject it. Sergeant Inman has done this once too often for my liking and is, I believe, now too old to mend his ways.' He looked directly at Inman. 'It's my intention to terminate your four weeks here and send you back to Hereford with the recommendation that you be RTU'd with a view to discharge. I'm sorry, but I . . .'

The CO was cut off in mid-sentence by the telephone. Picking it up, he listened intently for some time, then slammed it down again.

'The Iranian Embassy in London has just been seized by terrorists,' he said. 'Your Regiment is on stand-by. You're both to leave immediately for Hereford.' He closed the folder and handed it to Shannon when the latter stood smartly and approached the desk. Lieutenant-Colonel Fairworth smiled tightly at Inman.

'Lucky you,' he said softly.

'Thank you, sir!' Inman responded, snapping off a crisp salute, then gratefully turning away and following the excited Shannon out of the office. Once outside, the latter turned to his old mate and gave him a wicked grin.

'Fairworth wasn't kidding,' he said. 'You really *are* one lucky bastard.'

'Don't I know it,' Inman replied. 'So what's the story, Paddy?'

'As I'm already an expert sniper,' Shannon replied, 'which is why I was teaching a prat like you, I'm bound to be in the perimeter containment group. As for you, since you've just been swilled out of the Commando sniper course, you'll almost certainly be back with one of the assault groups, which places you in the front line of fire. Just where you belong, you fucking lunatic.'

'Trust a Paddy to recognize a soul mate. So when do we leave?'

'The Bedfords are being prepared right now. We pack up and move out within the hour.'

'Sounds like heaven,' Inman said as both men walked away from the HQ, revitalized by the thought of packing up and going back to their own world.

5

'As you all know by now,' the Controller said to his men in a briefing room in the Kremlin, the intelligence wing of the SAS HQ in Hereford, 'the Iranian Embassy was occupied this morning by six Iranian terrorists trained and armed in Baghdad. They're armed with two Skorpion W263 Polish sub-machine-guns, three Browning self-loading pistols, one .38 Astra revolver and five Russian RGD5 hand-grenades. As far as we know, they have a lot of ammunition.'

'We've got a lot of ammunition as well,' the CRW Red Team leader, Staff-Sergeant Bill Harrison, said. 'That's not our major anxiety, boss.'

'So what is?'

'Their motive.'

'Why?'

'Because the motive tells us how they might react.'

'Very good, Staff-Sergeant.' The Controller smiled in his quietly understated public-school manner. 'The stated purpose of their mission is to publicize the plight of Arabs in Iran and to demand the freedom of 92 political prisoners held in that country.'

'Is that generally believed?' asked the head of the Blue Team, Staff-Sergeant 'Jock' Thompson.

The Controller shook his head. 'No. It's our belief that Saddam Hussein, a gangster of a politician, wants back the eastern half of the Shatt-al-Arab boundary with Iran, ceded to that country in 1975. It's also our belief that following the successful Iranian seizure of the American Embassy in Tehran, Saddam is using the seizure of the Iranian Embassy in London as his own display of strength to the Arab world.'

'Who's in charge of negotiations with the terrorists?' Blue Team's Sergeant Inman asked, always keen to smell the meat of the matter.

'As this is a political matter, the operation is in the hands of the Cabinet Office Briefing Room, COBR – pronounced like the snake. This top-level committee also includes representatives of the police, MI5 and, of course, this Regiment. In other words, we have a direct channel to the top of the decision-making pyramid and operational links with the police at the location of the siege.'

'So *they* decide when we go in – not us,' the contentious sergeant said.

'Correct.'

Nothing about Inman bothered the Controller, even if it bothered a lot of others in the Regiment. In fact, the Controller's considerable respect for Inman's talents had compelled him to drag him back for special training in CRW skills. Though Inman had made no bones about hating the necessarily repetitive training in the 'killing house', the Controller had not been disappointed.

Inman, with his special brand of sharp-edged aggressiveness, had proved himself as a CRW natural. Now, though he was grinning in a challenging manner at the Controller, the latter was merely amused and responded with the simple, albeit deadly, facts.

'This being a political matter,' he said, 'we have to remain neutral and use force only when no other options are left. We'll be informed when that time comes. Meanwhile, it's the police who'll negotiate with the terrorists. Initially we remain on the sidelines.'

'We're supposed to be an anonymous Regiment, boss,' Staff-Sergeant Harrison said. 'Seems to me that if we go into that Embassy we'll be doing so right in front of TV cameras, radio commentators and the international news media. That puts us in the spotlight.'

'Again, we've no choice,' said the Controller with a shrug. 'Besides, the days when the Regiment only operated overseas are already over. For the past few years London has become a battleground for numerous Middle East terrorist groups, so we've no choice but to tackle them on home ground. If they wear civilian clothing, so will we; it's a new form of warfare.'

'Do you think the terrorists can be talked out of the Embassy by the police?' The question, surprisingly, came from Red Team's Lance-Corporal Phil McArthur, not normally noted for putting himself forward. Sitting beside his closest Red Team friends, Troopers Alan Pyle, Ken Passmore and Danny 'Baby Face' Porter, he was visibly embarrassed even as he asked the question. Danny, nick named 'Baby Face' because he looked like the cowboy hero Audie Murphy and was just as deadly, was embarrassed by nothing.

'Personally, I doubt it,' the Controller said. 'Those terrorists were making their plans in London when uncensored television reports of the Desert One disaster, in which the US Delta Force – widely viewed as our cousin – left eight dead in burning helicopters in their failed attempt to rescue American hostages from Tehran. The terrorists would almost certainly have seen those televised reports. To them, the

American disaster would have been a good omen. So, no, I don't think they'll be talked out of there.'

'What weapons will we have?' Jock Thompson asked.

'The Ingram?' Blue Team's Lance-Corporal 'Danny Boy' Reynolds asked, referring to the American 9mm sub-machine-gun normally favoured by the SAS CT teams.

'No,' the Controller replied. 'Since the joint SAS/GSG assault on the hijacked Lufthansa airliner at Mogadishu, we've been looking for a weapon that fires rapidly and precisely, but at low velocity, so that the bullets will hit the intended target without penetrating it and striking another. As excessive fire-power will result in a propaganda victory for the terrorists, we want this operation over as quickly as possible. We've therefore settled on the Heckler & Koch MP5.'

'Untried,' Blue Team's special sniper, Sergeant Pat 'Paddy' Shannon said bluntly.

'Untrue. It's been tried and proven excellent.'

'In what way?' Staff-Sergeant Harrison asked.

'Like the Ingram, it's small and compact – 5½ lb when empty; 27 inches in length. Unlike the Ingram, however, it fires from a closed bolt, which reduces the shift in balance when it's fired, thus giving it uncommon accuracy. For this reason, also, it rarely jams. Calibre, 9mm. Rate of fire, 800 rounds per minute. It offers a choice of single-shot, fully automatic or three-round burst fire, with an effective range of 200 yards. Fifteen- or twenty-round box magazine.'

'I read somewhere that this weapon *does* jam,' Harrison objected.

'Earlier models did. The latest model doesn't.'

'Ho, ho,' Inman said in his usual mocking manner.

The Controller just grinned. 'The weapon was made in West Germany. We know how bright the Germans are. They soon discovered that another, foreign-made bullet could yield unparalleled accuracy. Those bullets, however, were the culprits that caused the old-style magazine to jam. The problem was solved simply by making the magazine curved instead. It doesn't jam any more.'

'Let's hope not,' Inman said.

'What else will we be using?' Blue Team's Trooper 'Bobs-boy' Quayle asked.

'The Browning 9mm High Power handgun . . .'

'The good old 9-milly!' Bobs-boy crowed, referring to the thirteen-round weapon beloved of the SAS ever since its use in the famous Keeni Meeni assassination operations in Aden during the early 1960s.

'. . . and the Remington 870 pump-action shotgun, which we'll need to blast the locks from the doors of locked rooms. Also, plastic explosives and flash-bangs, the latter for their shock effect on the terrorists during the first few seconds of the siege, and CS gas grenades. To prevent you from wasting time donning gas masks during the attack, you'll put them on before the attack commences and wear them throughout the whole operation.'

'The flash-bangs and CS gas grenades could cause a fire inside the building,' Harrison pointed out.

'That's a chance we'll have to take,' the Controller replied. 'Apart from the sub-machine-guns, we have nothing more effective in such a confined space – particularly if we're masked against the gas and the terrorists aren't.'

'So what's the plan of action?' asked the baby-faced killer, Danny Porter.

'The police are negotiating with the terrorists at this moment,' the Controller said, 'and have so far succeeded in having a few of the hostages released. They are already being debriefed and will provide invaluable information about the state of mind of the terrorists, what weapons they have, and where they're holding the other hostages. The negotiations are also distracting the terrorists, and buying the police time, enabling the latter to bug the building and scan it with thermal imagers.'

'So what do we do while they're scanning the building?' Jock asked.

'You're in two teams: Red and Blue. The Red Team will be insinuated into the Royal College of Medical Practitioners, located right next door to the Embassy. This team will be headed by Captain Williams, your CRW instructor, and consist of twenty-four men. To avoid the press, you'll be transported from here by hired vans to the Regent's Park Barracks of the Household Cavalry, in Albany Street, where you will stay when not on alert. You will, however, when called out on alert or for daily training, be smuggled into the grounds of the college in the same Avis vans. From there you will make your way to the Forward Holding Area in the college by clambering unseen over the walls and rear gardens.'

'And once in the FHA?' Harrison asked.

'Your team's task is twofold. First, you have to be ready for an assault on the Embassy at ten minutes' notice, if the terrorists start killing. To be known as the "Immediate Action Plan", this will involve breaking in through the upper windows to clear the building room by room with CS gas and firearms, trusting that you can reach the hostages before the terrorists slaughter them. Your second task is to prepare for the "Deliberate Assault Plan", which is to be put into motion at a time chosen by us if and when the terrorists are exhausted and the location of the hostages is known.'

'Do we have much info on the Embassy?' Inman asked.

'Quite a lot, in fact. For a start, hostages are already being released and debriefed, which should produce a good deal of intelligence over the next few hours. Also, we have complete drawings which you'll be shown when the training commences.'

'And in the meantime?'

'Basically, what we're dealing with is a fortress situation. The Embassy is a very large, mid-terrace building on six floors, four of which are above ground. There are fifty rooms in all. It's to the advantage of the terrorists that the building can easily be defended front and rear because of the open spaces to either side of it. We're therefore considering a frontal charge, as well as abseiling from the roof onto the balconies along the front of the building. Before any final plan for that is made, however, and while more information about the inside of the Embassy is being received, our own Intelligence cell, aided by a member of the Embassy staff, is fabricating a model of the building. Based on this information, a full-scale hessian model of the Embassy's main rooms is already being constructed at Regent's Park Barracks, where an Embassy caretaker will describe the layout for us.'

'Any questions?'

'No.'

'Then let's go.'

Excited to be back in business, the men hurried out of the briefing room.

6

Because this was the first SAS operation to take place on British soil and, worse still, in full view of the media, the usual arming of the men and donning of the required dress prior to the operation was avoided. Instead, the men of Red Team were transported from Hereford to London in hired vans, all wearing civilian clothing like factory workers and none of them armed. Their weapons and equipment were transported separately in crates stacked high in furniture vans.

'I like travelling in style,' Alan Pyle said sardonically as he sauntered with the others up to the van parked in the holding area. 'It makes me feel right at home.'

'He's a Londoner,' his fellow trooper, Ken Passmore, explained to those with ears. He was a clear-headed, unprejudiced Geordie. 'I think that says it all.'

'Right,' his mate, Danny Boy, agreed, being from Bridlington, Humberside, which he often recalled with the deepest loathing. 'People from the South, as we all know, are born and bred rich. They *all* travel in Avis vans.'

'I've never been in one,' Bobs-boy said. He was from Rickmansworth, Hertfordshire, and had seen the odd Avis van, though no one thought it was really that unusual that he had never been in one. 'This will be my first time.'

'You're so sophisticated,' Alan told him.

'You think so?' Bobs-boy asked. 'I have to confess that I like the old 4 x 4 Bedford, so I might like the Avis.'

'What a fucking prat!' Corporal George 'GG' Gerrard whispered to his mate, Lance-Corporal Phil McArthur, as he swung the rear door of the van open. 'Straight off the farm!'

'Just get in the fucking van,' Phil replied, 'and let's go and find some action.'

'I trust we do,' grunted GG.

Strangely enough, as the van was carrying them along the M40 to London, the men broke with tradition by avoiding the customary 'bullshit' and speaking only when necessary. Perhaps this was due to the fact that this was not a long journey, that they were wearing civilian clothing and that they all had the feeling that they were already in action. By the time they had left the motorway, the men were absolutely silent. When the van eventually turned in through the guarded gates of Regent's Park Barracks, in Albany Street, they piled out and quickly made their way into the bleak, dusty barracks. Shocked by what they found on entering the dormitory chosen for them, they returned to the bullshit.

'I don't believe it,' GG groaned, taking in at a glance the dust on the brick window ledges and floor, between the rusty, steel-framed Army camp-beds with their battered, stained mattresses. 'It looks like a cowshed.'

'The Household Cavalry!' Phil snorted. 'I thought we'd be living like lords, but just look at this doss-house!'

'I bet *they* live like lords.'

'Who?'

'The Household Cavalry. They're probably in another part of the barracks, walking on thick carpets, sleeping in silk sheets, getting hand-jobs from maids in nothing but white aprons.'

'We have to basha down *here?*' Danny Boy could not believe it either. He had lived in many a hole in Humberside in his time, but this was the pits.

'I lived better in Notting Hill Gate,' Alan informed them, 'when I shared a flat with half-a-dozen kids who didn't know what a vacuum cleaner was and were too stoned to take a bath.'

'These toilets stink,' Baby Face announced from where he stood at the end of the dormitory. 'The water's come right up to the top and it's covered in brown slime.'

'Jesus Christ!' Bobs-boy said.

'God have mercy!' GG added.

'Are you men complaining?' Staff-Sergeant Jock Thompson asked, his shadow stretching out from his feet where he stood in the doorway, his thick arms folded across his broad chest, his face flushed and unsmiling.

'Not me!' GG said.

'I'm happy as Larry,' Bobs-boy said.

'These toilets stink,' Baby Face repeated, 'so they must need unblocking.'

'Then unblock them,' Jock said, 'and clean up this place. When you've done that, make up your bashas, unpack your kit, then go back out to the parking area to wait for the vans. If you're not out there in thirty minutes sharp, you'll all face a fine.'

'Yes, boss!' the men barked simultaneously, feeling blessed when Jock nodded grimly and departed once more.

'Phew!' Phil said softly. 'Well, lads, let's get to it.'

They made up their bashas on the rusty steel-framed beds, quickly dusted down the floors and windows – though the dust returned almost immediately – managed with much cursing to unblock the toilets, then went back out to the parking area, where Jock was waiting for them, just in time to greet the arrival of the furniture vans. When the vans braked to a halt, the men unloaded the crates of weapons and equipment, then carried them inside with much huffing and puffing.

'If we were in any other regiment,' GG complained, 'we'd have crap-hats to hump this stuff in for us. Trust the bloody SAS!'

'I blame it all on the Household Cavalry,' Phil said. 'Those bastards are probably watching us right now from their more luxurious quarters.'

'Having a good laugh,' Bobs-boy said.

'Spoilt bastards,' added Danny Boy.

'Stop whining!' Jock bawled, appearing out of nowhere and casting his enormous shadow over them as they humped the gear in. 'If I hear one more complaint from you lot, I'm going to start throwing fines around.'

'No complaints from me,' Bobs-boy said, struggling backwards with the crate being shared with Alan. 'I love unpacking things.'

'He's gone already,' Alan said, lowering his end of the crate, 'so you can put the crate down. When you've done so, wipe the brown from your nose. It's beginning to smell.'

'What?'

'Never mind.'

After opening the crates, the men stripped off their civvies and put on their CRW gear. This consisted of black CRW assault suits with felt pads in knees and elbows; flame-resistant underwear; GPV 25 wrap-around soft body armour with hard ceramic composite plates front and back; NBC hoods for protection against heat, dust and smoke (the men would not

56

be wearing helmets); and the 800gm S6 respirator with nosecup filter for protection against gases, aerosols and smoke; scratch-resistant, polycarbonate eyepieces, also resistant to chemical or solvent attack; tinted lenses for protection against the flash from stun grenades; and microphones mounted in front of the mouthpiece, to be linked by means of a communication harness to the assault team's radio transmitter.

'This is the part I hate most,' Bobs-boy said as he adjusted the CRW vest in the hope of being a little more comfortable. 'It always makes me feel a bit weird.'

'I agree,' Danny Boy said, slipping on his black, skin-tight aviator's gloves. 'This gear makes me feel evil.'

'You pair of ponces talked that way in the killing house,' GG said, ignoring the fact that he had said much the same thing at the same time, 'and got a rocket from that bastard Thompson. I'd keep quiet if I was you.'

'Hey, you lot!' Jock suddenly bawled, having just material-ized in the doorway. 'Are you ready or not?'

'Yes, boss!'

'Then let's move it!'

Leaving the spider, the men proceeded to the lecture hall, where they were divided into three teams – Red, Blue and the perimeter containment group, otherwise known as snipers, to be condenamed Zero Delta. They were then allocated their weapons, the armaments they received depending on which particular role they had been assigned in the forthcoming operation. While most of them were armed with the new Heckler & Koch MP5 sub-machine-gun and the standard-issue Browning 9mm High Power handgun, those in the perimeter containment teams led by Sergeant Shannon were given the L42A1 .303-inch bolt-action sniper rifle with tripod. A few members of the assault teams, tasked with breaking into the locked rooms of the Embassy, were given the Remington 870 pump-action shotgun. Some were put in charge of a variety of explosive devices, including frame charges and explosive door cutters. All of the men were also issued with spare magazines, ISFE, CS gas and MX5 stun grenades.

Finally, the equipment was distributed according to each man's assigned role in the operation. This included W.J. Crow lightweight aluminium assault ladders; sledgehammers, axes, wrecking bars, glasscutters and grappling hooks.

Once dressed and armed, the men were officially on stand-by and ready to go.

The Controller gave them a briefing in the barracks, where diagrams of the Embassy, including the layout of the individual rooms, were pinned on blackboards. The Controller indicated the drawing under discussion with a wooden pointer and the men listened intently while sitting on the edge of their beds, wearing their complete CRW gear. To an outsider, the gathering would have made a bizarre, menacing sight.

'I believe the planning team has covered every possible angle,' the Controller told them, 'though naturally, in a highly volatile situation like this, we can't be too sure, so you'll have to be prepared for the unexpected.' He paused to let these words sink in. 'The attack will focus on a single objective: to rescue the hostages from the Iranian Embassy, if necessary. In order to do this, Red Team will clear the top half of the building, from the second to the fourth floor. Blue Team will tackle the lower half from the basement and garden, upwards to the first floor. Blue Team will also handle evacuation procedures.'

'How do we enter?' Staff-Sergeant Harrison asked.

'Red Team will drop two abseil teams, each of four men, in separate waves from the roof, down to the second-floor balcony at the back of the building.' The Controller tapped a photographic enlargement of the balcony with his pointer. 'Once on the balcony, Red Team will break in through those three big windows.' He indicated the windows with his pointer. 'While this first group is thus engaged, another group will be tasked with attacking the third floor, descending from the roof by ladder onto a sub-roof at the rear, known as the lighting area.' He indicated the area as shown on one of the drawings of the Embassy. 'At the same time, at fourth-floor level, a third group will blast a way in through the skylight, direct from the roof.'

'And Blue Team?' asked Jock, that team's leader.

'Blue Team will be in charge of the garden-level basement, along with the ground floor and first floor. As far as we can ascertain from the layouts, what will be required is an explosive charge to be put in the French windows overlooking the ground-floor terrace at the back. A similar bit of surgery will be required on the front, first-floor balcony window leading to the Minister's office. Access to that balcony isn't a problem since it adjoins the balcony of the Royal College of Medical Practitioners, already being prepared for a take-over by us.'

'What might be a problem,' Harrison pointed out, 'is finding the explosive power needed to demolish those windows. They are, as I recall, made of specially reinforced glass installed originally on SAS advice.'

The wisecrack copped a few laughs and sardonic comments from the men. When they had settled down again, the Controller said: 'It didn't escape our attention that the windows had been installed on our advice and are particularly tough to crack. However, we believe that a special frame explosive, matching that of the window frame to be demolished, will do the job. At the critical moment, the explosive will be carried from balcony to balcony and lifted on to the target – like a jacket fitted onto a tailor's dummy, as it were. I'm sure you can manage it.'

'What else is Blue Team responsible for?' Jock wanted to know.

'For the firing of CS gas canisters into the rear second-floor windows at the beginning of the attack. At the end of the attack, it's Blue Team that will hold an undiplomatic reception party in the garden.'

'A *what?*' Bobs-boy asked.

'An *un*diplomatic reception,' the Controller repeated with a grin. 'That means you will manhandle everyone found in the Embassy – terrorists and hostages alike – out into the back garden and there search them, bind their hands and feet, lay them face down on the grass, and proceed to question them until you've ascertained who's a terrorist and who a hostage. You will do so with dispatch, tolerating no protest and being a little rough if necessary. That's why it's called an undiplomatic reception.'

'Neat,' the trooper said.

'Who's orchestrating the operation?' asked Jock.

'A command group led by myself and a controller, operating from a sixth-floor flat overlooking the rear of the Embassy, out of sight of the journalists.'

'How long do you think the siege will last, boss?'

'I've no idea. I only know that those men are determined, so it could last for a long time.'

'What do we do while we wait?'

'Immediately after this briefing you'll pack your kit and prepare to be insinuated into the Forward Holding Area in the Royal College of Medical Practitioners, located next door to the Embassy. While you wait on stand-by, you'll familiarize yourselves with both the Immediate Action Plan and the Deliberate Assault Plan, training with full kit and studying every photograph, drawing, report we've got on the terrorists and their unfortunate hostages. Another hostage has been released since our arrival here and that means even more information on the terrorists and their arms and state of mind. Also, a replica of the Embassy has been constructed in the Forward Holding Area and you'll use that to familiarize yourselves with the building and your own place in both the Deliberate Assault Plan and the Immediate Action Plan. As the former becomes more defined, its most important elements will be fed into the latter: the scheme to storm the building as a prompt response to any murders. The learning process will therefore be non-stop – at least until you're either stood down for good or called to implement the attack plan. Rest assured, you'll be busy. Any more questions?'

When his question was followed by the silent shaking of heads, the Controller said: 'All right, men, let's go.'

Heavily burdened with weapons, sledgehammers, ladders, abseiling ropes and other equipment, the men in the sinister black CRW outfits marched out of the dormitory and clambered into the vans parked outside. The convoy eventually rolled out of Regent's Park Barracks and headed south-westwards for Princes Gate.

7

Once in the Royal College of Medical Practitioners, at 14 Princes Gate, the men of Red Team clambered up onto the gently sloping roof in full CRW gear, then made their way stealthily across to the adjoining roof of the Embassy, where they quietly tied the required number of abseiling ropes to the chimneys, then left the rest coiled up beside each chimney.

When this was done, they crossed back to the college and made their way back down to the rooms designated as their Forward Holding Area. There, the learning process for Red Team did indeed become non-stop in the frustrating periods between false alerts and being stood down again. This happened many times during their first twenty-three hours in the college.

When on stand-by, the men of Red Team were allowed to strip off their heavy CRW outfits to wear casual clothing. But as each new terrorist deadline approached, they had to get into their fighting equipment and out onto the roof to prepare to go into action, on a radio message, 'London Bridge', at four minutes' notice. They were, however, stood down repeatedly, which caused much frustration.

'This is driving me crazy,' grumbled Phil McArthur as he divested himself of his CRW gear for the fourth time. 'Why the hell don't they let us cross that roof and get on with the job?'

'It's because they're trying to talk the terrorists out instead of sending us in,' Staff-Sergeant Harrison informed him.

'Damned Met!' Trooper Alan Pyle said in his oddly distracted drawl, showing no real irritation. 'They're only good for directing the traffic and they're not good at that. What *are* they good at?'

In fact, he was recalling how, from the roof of the college, he had been able to look all the way along to the metal scaffolding and canvas marquee of the press enclosure hastily constructed in Hyde Park, as well as the numerous vans, cars and trailers of the police and media, with TV and communications cables snaking across the road. Down on the street, directly in front of the adjoining Embassy, inside an area cordoned off with coloured tape, a plain-clothes policeman had been negotiating with the terrorists, speaking English when conveying his message via the hostages Sim Harris and PC Lock, or through an interpreter when speaking directly to a terrorist. It had looked like a circus down there, but nothing seemed to be happening.

'All they do,' Alan continued, 'is talk, talk, talk, while those bloody terrorists create one deadline after another, just stringing the bloody coppers along. They should send us in right now.'

'They can't make up their minds because the terrorists' demands keep changing,' Jock explained.

'That's exactly what Alan meant,' Baby Face said. 'Those terrorists are calling all the shots, so we should go in right now.'

'I agree,' Sergeant Inman said. 'The more we wait, the more hysterical they'll get and the more dangerous that makes them. Also, the more we wait, the more they'll expect us, which loses us the element of surprise.'

'Right,' Baby Face said. 'They're thinking it's early days yet and we should move while they're thinking that. We could take them before they blink.'

'You're a pair of fucking warmongers, you two,' Jock broke in. 'You're only interest is in having a little mix and tasting their blood. Your interest stops right there.'

'And you?' Inman asked.

'What about me?' Jock replied.

'Whose interest do you have at heart, since you're sounding so noble?'

'Don't be insolent, Sergeant. I'm still the senior NCO. You try to cut me with that sharp tongue and I'll tear it out of your throat.'

'That's pulling rank, Staff-Sergeant.'

'I treat a mad dog like a mad dog.'

'I'm just saying that the element of surprise is all we've got here – and we're losing it fast.'

Jock nodded, showing no animosity. 'Maybe you're right, pal. Who knows? You just might be.'

The first message about the occupation had been received by phone at the *Guardian* newspaper. Conveyed from the terrorist leader, by now known by all as Salim, his real name, via the hostage journalist Mustafa Karkouti, it stated that the terrorists had occupied the Embassy for their 'human and legitimate rights', which were 'freedom, autonomy and recognition of the Arabistan people'. The second phone message, conveyed by Karkouti to a Senior Deputy Editor of the BBC's External Services, was a clarification that the terrorists were from Iran – not Iraq as had been widely believed – and a demand for the release of 91 prisoners being held in Arabistan.

At four-thirty p.m. on the first day the terrorists had released a female Iranian hostage, wrongly thinking, because she had fainted, that she was pregnant. Shortly after the woman's release, police activity outside the Embassy was intensified, with cordons completely ringing the area, the nearby main road, Kensington Gore, barred to traffic between the Albert Hall and Knightsbridge Barracks, and a carefully guarded press enclosure created near Exhibition Road.

A Police Forward Operations Room, Alpha Control, was set up in the Royal School of Needlework at 25 Princes Gate, from where all police and military activity was controlled.

By six o'clock all the buildings around the Embassy had been evacuated and the Metropolitan Police had begun speaking directly to the terrorists, either by phone or through the Embassy windows, in English and Arabic.

During the first of those conversations, Salim stated that if his demand for the release of the prisoners in Arabistan was not met by noon the following day, he would blow up the Embassy and all inside it.

At eleven-thirty that same night, another hostage, Dr Afrouz, the Embassy's chargé d'affaires, telephoned the Foreign Ministry in Tehran, to explain that the terrorists were all Iranian citizens, Muslim brothers, and that they would end the siege when the Iranian government agreed to a degree of autonomy for Arabistan.

Nothing had happened during the first night, but in the early hours of Day Two, Thursday, 1 May, another message from Oan-Ali informed a BBC News Desk deputy editor that the British hostages and other non-Iranian hostages would not be harmed, though the deadline for the safety of the others was still valid.

'Meanwhile,' Staff-Sergeant Harrison told his frustrated Red Team as they crouched in full CRW battle gear, surrounded by weapons, abseiling equipment and sledgehammers, on the windy roof of the college, 'thermal imagers and bugging devices planted in the walls of the Embassy have revealed that the hostages, men and women alike, are presently being held in Room 9A on the second floor.'

Shortly after this revelation, the audio-surveillance devices picked up the sound of a terrorist firing a threatening burst into the ceiling of Room 9A, causing some of the women to scream. This was followed by a phone call from one of the hostages, BBC sound recordist Sim Harris, explaining that his fellow hostage, BBC news organizer Chris Cramer, was writhing in increasing pain from the symptoms of a virulent dysentery he had picked up in Rhodesia, and needed a doctor.

The police refused the request.

A second request met with the same response, though this time the police cleverly suggested that Harris should try persuading the terrorists to release his friend. Harris did so, and at eleven-fifteen that morning the Embassy door was opened to enable Cramer to stagger to a waiting ambulance.

'Those two hostages,' Harrison explained, 'when questioned by the police, revealed a great deal about what's going on inside the Embassy.'

'So?' Baby Face asked.

Harrison sighed at the trooper's ignorance. 'With each new scrap of information from a hostage, our assault plans are changing. That's why we never stop rehearsing – and why each one is different. As for Cramer, he's told us a lot. So you lot are now in for lots of work.'

'What kind of work?'

'More rehearsals of revised situations. They should keep you busy.'

'Gee, thanks,' GG said.

Ten minutes after the noon deadline, Salim phoned to say, in his poor English, that he was giving the Iranian Government until two that afternoon to meet his demands. When that deadline also passed with no response from the Iranian Government, there was no sound of an explosion inside the Embassy.

'It seems that Salim has changed his mind,' Staff-Sergeant Harrison told them after speaking on the radio phone to the Controller, who was based for the time being in Alpha Control at 25 Princes Gate. 'He's holding out for more than they're offering and they're going to call his bluff.'

'Calling his bluff could get a hostage killed,' Inman responded. 'Those fucking Arabs aren't playing games.'

'Nor are we, Sarge. We're just engaged in a bit of the old in-and-out: a little cry of protest here, a sigh of gratitude there; first cold, then hot; now advancing, now retreating; giving a little, then taking some away; stepping forward, then back again, maybe turning in circles. It's what's known as a protracted negotiation and the Met are good at it.'

'I'm glad they're good at something,' Alan chipped in. 'I was giving up hope.'

'Oh, they're good,' Harrison insisted. 'The police negotiators are very good indeed and have, I believe, managed to cool things down a little. All is calm for the moment.'

But things were hotting up outside. There, beyond the police cordons, nearly 400 Khomeini loyalists demonstrated and were met by abuse from hordes of British louts howling derision and shaking their fists. Many were arrested.

That afternoon, the terrorists again insisted that if the Iranian Government acceded to their modest demands, the siege would end peacefully. Again the Government did not respond. This encouraged Salim to ask for three Arab ambassadors – from Jordan, Iraq and Algeria – to arrange for a plane to take him and his fellow terrorists out of Britain, when they were ready to go.

Shortly after eight p.m., when the police were drilling holes in the walls of the Embassy to insert more audio-surveillance probes, two of the hostages, Mustafa Karkouti and PC Lock, appeared at a first-floor window, both covered by a terrorist gunman, to ask what the noises were. The police denied that they were responsible and another night passed peacefully.

Throughout that tense first twenty-three hours, the SAS's Red Team had been repeatedly put on alert, each time having to don their full CRW outfits, collect their weapons and equipment, including abseiling ropes and harness, then go out onto the roof of the college, ready to clamber over onto the roof of the Embassy. Each time, to their immense frustration, they were made to stand down again.

They were, however, given no rest. Instead, they studied every photograph, drawing, report and other scrap of information fed to them about the people next door. Also, with the helpful narration of a former Embassy caretaker, they repeatedly studied a plywood scale model of the Embassy, working out just how they would enter, what routes they would take once inside, and what specific targets, or rooms, each team would be responsible for clearing. Their positions and routes were demonstrated with the aid of toy soldiers placed at various points outside and in the corridors and rooms of the scale model.

'I feel like a right dick doing this,' Alan said.

'You *are* a right dick,' Phil told him, 'so you've nothing to lose.'

'Toy soldiers and doll's houses,' Trooper Ken Passmore said. 'It takes me back to my school days.'

'You played with *doll's houses?*' Phil asked him.

'And wore skirts,' Ken replied. 'I managed to get into the SAS by flashing my knickers at the drill instructors. It's a common girl's trick.'

'Do we go left or right at the end of that corridor?' Baby Face asked, pointing at the model of the Embassy and looking as sombre as always.

'Left,' Harrison said, then offered a loud sigh. 'It's nice to know I've got *one* trooper with concentration. Any more questions, lads?'

'Yes,' Phil said. 'Who do I have to fuck to get off this job?'

'Ken Passmore!' they all cried out in chorus, being desperate for light relief.

This they did not get, however. After twenty-three hours of being called out onto the roof of the college, fully armed and dressed, and with abseiling equipment, ladders and explosives to hand, only to be stood down again and returned to yet more planning around the scale model, the men of Red Team were not only immensely exhausted, but fast running out of patience.

They returned to the Regent's Park Barracks to catch up on their sleep.

Blue Team arrived at the FHA at three-thirty a.m. on Day Three. Like Red Team, they had been transported from Bradbury Lines to the Regent's Park Barracks by van, then moved on to the college in furniture vans. While Red Team caught up with a little sleep, the twenty-four-man Blue Team, headed by an SAS captain, took over the responsibility for the Immediate Action Plan and, like Red Team, were compelled to spend hours studying the scale model of the Embassy next door. They, too, were called out more than once, then stood down again.

'It's driving me bonkers,' Danny Boy said after the third alert and stand-down. 'Up on that fucking roof, all set to roll, then called back down again. What the hell are they playing at?'

'The terrorists keep changing their demands,' Jock informed him. 'Oan-Ali threatens to blow up the building, so we're called out on alert. Then instead of blowing the building up, he releases a hostage, so we're stood down again. It's a form of psychological warfare and it's very effective.'

'It's certainly affecting *me*,' GG complained. 'If we're stood down once more, I'll throw myself off this fucking roof.'

'Goodbye,' Danny Boy said.

'Fuck you,' GG shot back.

'I don't mind,' Trooper 'Bobs-boy' Quayle said. 'At least they're keeping us busy.'

'I'd rather keep myself busy with a pint of bitter,' GG said. 'All this stop-go's no good for me.'

'Stop whining, you lot,' Jock told them. 'I'm fed up with the sound of your voices. Now let's go back down.'

'Yes, boss!' they all sang in unison, picking up their weapons and equipment and following their leader back down the stairs to the FHA below.

By this time, confirmation had been received from the audio-surveillance team that the hostages were indeed in Room 9A on the second floor.

Shortly after this information was conveyed to the police and SAS, Salim appeared at the window, pointing a pistol at the head of a terrified hostage, the Embassy's cultural attaché, Dr Abul Fazi Ezzatti, whom he threatened to kill unless he was allowed to talk to the media by telephone or telex.

'I'm sorry, Salim,' the police negotiator told the terrorist leader, 'but we can't do that just yet. We need time to set it up.'

'Liars!' the Iranian screamed.

Nevertheless, instead of killing the visibly distressed hostage, he merely pushed him roughly aside, out of sight behind the window frame. Intelligence later discovered that the terrified Ezzatti had then collapsed, foaming at the mouth.

'The terrorist leader is clearly reaching the end of his tether,' the Controller told the exasperated men of the Blue Team shortly after they had been called down yet again. 'My personal belief is that the killing will start soon and we'll have to go in there.'

'I certainly hope so,' the action-hungry Sergeant Inman said. 'I'm brain-dead from sitting here.'

Another deadline was set for a few hours later. This time the terrorists demanded a talk with someone from the BBC, which they would conduct through their hostage Sim Harris. Though the police at first refused, more death threats from the terrorists finally made them relent.

That afternoon a managing editor of BBC TV news was produced to stand outside the Embassy and conduct a conversation with the sound recordist, who was standing at a first-floor window with Oan-Ali aiming a gun at his head from behind the curtain.

'This time,' the Controller told his gathered Red and Blue Teams, 'Salim has demanded a coach to take his fellow gunmen, the hostages, and at least one unnamed Arab ambassador to Heathrow. The non-Iranian hostages, he claims, will be released there. The aircraft will then take the terrorists, their hostages and the unnamed ambassador to an unspecified Middle East country. Once there, the hostages and ambassador will be released. Salim also wants a communiqué about his aims and grievances to be broadcast in Britain this evening.'

'He'll be bloody lucky,' Jock said.

He was right. That evening the BBC gave Salim's demands only the briefest of mentions. Though expressing his outrage through Sim Harris, the terrorist leader again took no action against his hostages.

'I know you men are getting more frustrated at all these false alarms,' the Controller said at another meeting in the FHA, 'but I have at least obtained the promise that if there's no peaceful outcome – and I doubt that there will be – then, when we're finally committed, there'll be no last-minute change of mind. Once we start, we don't stop.'

'Any increase in intelligence,' Red Team's experienced Sergeant Inman asked, 'since our briefing back in Bradbury Lines?'

'Yes. Most important was the evacuation of the BBC Television News organizer, Chris Cramer, with severe stomach cramps, at eleven-twenty a.m. yesterday. Cramer was able to confirm that PC Lock still has his pistol; that there are six terrorists – not five as initially believed; and that each terrorist carries two hand-grenades as well as small arms.'

'Is it true, as rumour has it, that the terrorists have wired the building for a doomsday explosion?'

'The terrorists certainly made that claim. Unfortunately, neither of the two released hostages could either confirm or deny that they actually did it. The hostages spent most of their time locked in Room 9, on the second floor, while the terrorists wandered freely about the building – so it could indeed have been so wired without the hostages' knowledge.'

'Does Salim still want the release of those 92 prisoners in Iran.'

'No. He phoned the negotiators yesterday evening to say he just wanted a bus with curtained windows to carry his men and the hostages to an airport, and an aircraft to fly the rest of the party, including the Iranian hostages, to the Middle East. However, as he also wanted the ambassadors of Iraq,

Algeria and Jordan, as well as a Red Cross representative, to be present during the transfer, that's not likely to happen.'

'Which is why we're now examining alternatives to a fortress attack,' Jock said shrewdly.

'Correct, Jock,' said the Controller. 'Salim's increasingly jittery and indecisive, which means he could start killing soon. If he does, we'll be called in. Meanwhile, we're continuing to install audio-surveillance probes and 8mm high-grain microphone probes in the walls of the Embassy.'

'They must be able to hear the sound of the drilling,' Inman said.

The Controller shrugged and grinned. 'The first time we drilled, the terrorists sent PC Lock and a Syrian journalist to the window to ask the police if they were making the noise. According to the released hostage, Chris Cramer, when the police denied the charge but the noise continued, the quick-witted PC Lock told the terrorists it was the sound of a London mouse.'

This provoked a few snorts of mirth.

'Good man,' GG said.

'What's Whitehall's attitude at the moment?' Harrison asked. 'Are they the ones holding us back?'

'Yes,' the Controller replied. 'Reportedly, the Home Secretary, Foreign Office representative Douglas Hurd, and Metropolitan Police Commissioner Sir David McNee have between them opted for a policy of maximum patience. While this excludes capitulation to the terrorists' demands, it also rules out any pre-emptive assault by us, unless a hostage is murdered.'

'That strikes me as leaving the initiative to the terrorists,' Inman said, sounding disgruntled.

'Maybe. But it can also be viewed as a policy of psychological attrition under the guise of negotiation. Short of sending us in on an assault, there's not much else they can do.'

'But I *want* to go in,' Inman insisted.

'Too bad,' Harrison said.

Inman looked directly at the Controller. 'So do you think, boss, that the terrorists will surrender peacefully?'

The Controller shook his head. 'No. It's not in their culture. Sooner or later they'll do some serious damage, then you'll get your chance, Sergeant.'

At that moment a message from the FHA below came through on the Controller's VHF/UHF handheld transceiver. When it ended, he turned to his men and said tersely: 'Another hostage is being released right now. Let's have a look.'

Hurrying to the edge of the roof, the men all looked obliquely at the cordoned-off area directly in front of the adjoining Embassy. It was eight-fifteen. Darkness was falling. Across the road, in Hyde Park, the canvas marquee of the press enclosure was bathed in floodlight. Picking their way through the tangle of cables and clambering boldly up the metal scaffolding around the marquee were many press photographers eager for a good shot of the emerging hostage. Closer to the Embassy, on the road at both sides of the area cordoned off by police barricades strung with coloured tapes, two 100-foot mobile gantries towered over the clutter of police vans, squad cars, trailers and ambulances. The restricted area itself, directly in front of the Embassy, was ringed with police. Isolated in the middle of the ring, but close to the front door of the Embassy, was a plain-clothes police negotiator with his civilian interpreter.

From the roof of the college, the Controller and his men were unable to see the front door of the Embassy, but they saw a lot of heads turning in that direction as a beam of light fell over the police negotiator and his colleague, indicating that the front door had just opened. A long, tense silence followed.

The Controller and his men leaned farther forward over the parapet of the college roof, straining to see who was emerging from the adjoining front door. The sound of shouting could be heard. The negotiator shouted something back and this was translated into Arabic by his interpreter.

Eventually, after what seemed like a long time, a woman came into view, walking from the hidden front door of the Embassy to the waiting negotiator. She spoke to him. A couple of police medics then rushed up to her, took hold of her by the arms and led her back to one of the parked ambulances. After being taken to hospital for a check-up, she would be passed on to the Metropolitan Police for debriefing and interrogation regarding what was happening inside the Embassy.

No sooner had the woman been rushed away than the sound of a door slamming was heard. Simultaneously, the light beaming onto the road from the front door of the Embassy blinked out. The police negotiator then hurried back to the senior officers grouped outside an HQ trailer parked at the far side of the road. When the negotiator passed on the message given to him by the released female hostage, the officers hurried away in different directions.

The Controller instantly called the HQ trailer on his hand-held transceiver, asking what was happening down below. He was informed that the woman was an Embassy secretary, Mrs Hiyech Sanei Kanji, who had been released solely in order to pass on another message from the terrorist leader. After hearing the message, the Controller passed it on to his own men.

'If the terrorist demands aren't broadcast,' he told them, 'they'll kill a hostage.'

All the men stiffened slightly, as if galvanized, then Inman, the most enthusiastic of all, asked: 'Does that mean we go in?'

The Controller dashed his hopes by shaking his head gravely. 'No,' he said. 'Mrs Thatcher has just endorsed the agreed strategy of maximum patience. That means we stand down again.'

'Shit!' the sergeant exploded, glancing down in disgust at the floodlit road in front of the Embassy.

Wearily, the men picked up their weapons and equipment, then made their way down from the college roof and to the FHA, from where they would be driven back to the Regent's Park Barracks for sleep, then more training.

8

The barracks were bleak, draughty and dusty, with frequently blocked toilets and no hot water. When not sleeping on their steel-framed camp-beds, the men were subjected to a seemingly endless succession of intelligence briefings from the 'green slime', repeated lessons about the assault plans with the scale model of the Embassy, and further anti-terrorist training. Some of the latter was being done in other locations in London, notably abseiling from the roof of Pearl House, a police residence in Pimlico.

Frustrating though all of this retraining was, it was made even more so by the fact that, since it was being conducted in the heart of the city, most of it, apart from the abseil training, had to be confined to boring lectures, rather than the physical skills. The men suffered such lectures in the freezing cold of a large, draughty room in the barracks, most of them muttering their resentment, when not actually shivering with cold.

'Bear in mind,' the Royal Army Medical Corps psychologist informed them, 'that a siege situation will always produce what is known as transference, which begins with mutual terror or revulsion and ends in mutual dependence, even friendship. Though the hostages may at first fear the gunmen, eventually they will come to feel that they are all in this thing together. Should negotiations be protracted, the hostages will come to resent the authorities outside the building and blame them for the lack of progress. From this will spring empathy, even sympathy for the terrorists, and eventually a friendship based on total dependence.

'When this transference occurs, the behaviour of hostage and terrorist alike will become even more unpredictable and dangerous. For this reason, when you forcibly enter a building under siege, you will be compelled to treat both in exactly the same way, making no attempt to distinguish between them. For this reason, also, when you clear the building, those rescued, hostage and terrorist alike, will *not* be driven directly away to prison, police station or hospital, but will be subjected immediately to an appropriate reception outside the building. This means being bound hand and foot, laid face down on the ground, then interrogated until adequate proof of identity or loyalties has been received. The hostages will then be separated from the terrorists and removed for debriefing, which will include psychiatric treatment to ensure that their emotional links to the terrorists are completely broken. This is not always easy.'

'Easier than attacking a building under siege,' Baby Face muttered. 'Those psychos have got jam on it.'

Baby Face was a natural soldier, a quiet, shy young man who had been born with the instincts of a killer and lived for the Regiment. Born and raised in Kingswinford, in the West Midlands, where he had led a life of almost total anonymity until reaching the age to enter the Army, he had joined up as soon as he could. Once in, he knew just what he wanted to do, which was apply for the legendary SAS. Naturally, he passed the notoriously tough Selection and Training stages with flying colours and soon found himself in Northern Ireland, where he was involved in surveillance from OPs in south Armagh and in highly dangerous CRW operations in the Catholic ghettos, using a Q car. Danny had made his first killings there, sometimes with the renowned 'double tap', at which he was an expert, other times in full-scale assaults with other SAS soldiers against IRA supporters in well-defended blocks of flats. Either way he had learned to shoot to kill without thinking twice.

Now, sitting in this draughty hall and compelled to listen to boring lectures, he distracted himself with thoughts of previous SAS engagements – a fire-fight with PIRA terrorists in rural Armagh; his lone killing of a Republican gunman on the roof of a housing estate in the Falls – or with thoughts of his family and friends. But the hard truth was that for him the former always took precedence over the latter.

'Communications,' said the lecturer from Royal Signals, Catterick, interrupting Baby Face's reverie, 'is possibly the most important aspect of any CRW operation. The nature of communications, or the lack thereof, can subtly sway the terrorists' thinking and behaviour. As for the men on the ground, full and adequate communications are of vital strategic importance and therefore cannot be ignored. For this purpose we have now developed a wide range of communications equipment suitable for short-range contact in siege situations. These would include everything from the standard-issue microprocessor-based tactical radio, the PRC 319, to the Davies Communications CT100 communications harness. The latter comprises an electronic ear-defender headset with earphone for the team radio – the CT100E – and a socket for connection to the CT100L body-worn microphone. It is therefore ideal for hostage-rescue work.

'Though the ear-defender is so designed as to restrict high-pressure sound from gunfire and grenade explosions, it allows normal speech to pass, including reception at all times from the assault team radio. It is, of course, a body-worn microphone with a front-mounted press-to-talk button which is disabled when the microphone is attached to the S6 respirator.

'Other items of similar CRW importance might be the Davies Communications M135b covert microphone and covert ear-worn receiver; various hand-held transceivers operating in the VHF/UHF frequency range and with built-in encryption facilities, such as the Landmaster III range from Pace Communications; and the Hagen Morfax Covert SKH, or surveillance communications harness, comprising a miniature microphone and earphone. In addition we have . . .'

'Dogshit,' Inman whispered into Baby Face's right ear. 'That's all any of this means to me. I'm already done in by that bastard droning on and on. What the hell are we doing sitting here when we could be on the roof of the Embassy, at least listening in? I've been through all this crap before and don't need reminding.'

'Yeah,' Baby Face replied in his soft manner. 'I know what you mean, Sarge.'

'Right. I know you do. You and me, kid, we know what we want – and what we *don't* want is this shit.'

'That's right, Sarge, we don't. What we want is to get off our backsides and abseil down those walls. We want to get inside.'

'Dead right, we do. We're forced to sit here and swallow this lot when we could be out there solving the problem. Abseil down the walls, blast the windows out, chuck in a couple of good old flash-bangs, fill the rooms with a cloud of CS gas and then go in after the bastards. We'd have them lying face down on the rear lawn before they knew what was happening.'

'I think you're right, Sarge.'

Baby Face revered Inman as one of the best soldiers in the Regiment, despite the fact that he was also known as a troublemaker. Although he hardly looked it, Inman was two years short of forty and had put in more hard experience with the SAS than anyone apart from Staff-Sergeant Richard 'Dead-eye' Parker, who was now with D Squadron. He was a hard man with a low boredom threshold, which made him volatile and unpredictable when not in action. Nevertheless, he loved the Regiment, respected its best soldiers, irrespective of rank, and had a particular fondness for young Danny for that very reason. He knew that, like himself, Baby Face could not stand inactivity and wanted to get the hell out of the barracks and back to the Embassy.

Let the kid loose in that building and you just couldn't lose, he thought to himself as he looked at the cherubic young trooper.

'Intelligence is, of course, one of the most important aspects of a siege situation,' the Kremlin-based 'green slime' instructor informed them as they sagged in their hard wooden chairs in the draughty, dusty dormitory being used as a lecture hall, 'and it is, of course, based largely on surveillance. As I'm sure you can imagine, the nature of surveillance in a siege situation is very different from that undertaken in an OP or from a Q car. As the prime difficulty in a siege situation is the building under siege, the major concern is to find out, before any assault is launched, what's being said and done inside. Electronic surveillance is therefore the order of the day and for that we have a variety of highly advanced listening and viewing instruments for which brick walls and closed windows are no problem.

'First and foremost is the Surveillance Technology Group range of systems, including an audio-surveillance lens and high-grain microphone probe, only 8mm in diameter, that can be coupled to any combination of tape recorder, 35mm camera or closed-circuit TV system and will monitor conversations through walls and other partitions, including reinforced windows. Even better is the same company's laser surveillance system, which consists of a tripod-mounted transmitter that directs an invisible beam onto the window of the target house, collecting the modulated vibrations created on the glass by the conversation going on inside. The modulated beam then bounces back to an optical receiver which converts it into audio signals. Those in turn are filtered, amplified and converted into clear conversations which can be monitored through headphones and recorded for subsequent examination. Thermal imaging is, of course, another viable option when darkness falls and it can be . . .'

'Jesus!' Trooper Alan Pyle hissed melodramatically. 'Will this torment never end?'

Unlike Baby Face, who spent more time thinking about fighting with the SAS than anything else, most of the younger SAS men banished the boredom of the lectures with predictably idealized thoughts of sex with wives, girlfriends, busty tabloid beauties and film and TV actresses. The more experienced hands, such as Phil and GG, tried gamely to forget sex and concentrate on their training, but the lectures were a soporific that rendered even them drowsy and so all the more prone to lustful fantasies.

'I wouldn't mind if we could leave these barracks at night,' Danny Boy said, relaxing on his camp-bed, 'to go out and pick up a bird in Camden Town. But being stuck here, night after night, is like being in prison.'

'Or a monastery,' Bobs-boy said.

'There speaks the man of God,' said Alan in his sardonic drawl, 'from the depths of experience.'

'An experienced wanker, more like,' said Ken derisively.

'Check your own mattress,' Bobs-boy retorted.

'My mattress, which was stained, is now soaked night and day,' the unembarrassed Ken came back without hesitation. 'I'm overloaded with tip-top sperm.'

'Have you noticed,' Alan asked, 'how the more those bloody instructors drone on, the more you start falling asleep and the more your head fills with horny thoughts?'

'Boredom breeds lust,' said Bobs-boy mock gravely.

'I just want to get back to Princes Gate,' Baby Face solemnly informed them, 'and into that Embassy. That's what we're here for.'

'We should be so lucky,' Inman said, stretched out on the adjacent camp-bed. It's not going to happen.'

'I think we will,' Baby Face insisted. 'In the next day or two. I'm sure of it.'

'Let us pray,' GG said lugubriously.

'Explosives,' the Royal Army Ordnance Corps demolition expert informed them at the next lecture, 'are almost certainly the most vital tools in any assault on a building being held by terrorists. Because that building also contains civilian hostages, the need for a precise knowledge of explosives is paramount. Obvious points of entry to such a building are doors, windows, and skylights, most of which will have to be forced with tools, weapons or, in the case of reinforced windows and skylights, with carefully calibrated quantities of explosive. As you all know by now – or *should* know by now – there are two types of explosive: low explosives, such as gunpowder, where the detonation is by burning; and high explosives, which the RAOC favours, where the charge is set off by an initiator. One reason we favour high explosives is that contrary to popular belief they're relatively insensitive – which prevents premature detonation – and resistant to heat and humidity. Among the best in current use are plastic explosives such as PETN, RDX, Semtex, Amatol and TNT. For the particular purposes of the kind of siege in which you are presently involved, we have developed what is known as a frame charge. This is an explosive in strip form that can be used for blowing precision holes through doors and brick-work, though it's infinitely more useful as an explosive shaped to a window frame for blowing out heavily reinforced windows. With regard to the way in which such a rapid-entry device is used . . .'

'Did he say premature detonation or premature ejaculation?' Alan asked when they were back in their temporary spider. 'Or am I just going mad?'

'I'd call it just finding your true self,' Ken replied.

'It's the boredom,' Phil explained. 'It's so bad, we're hallucinating. When that RAOC prat was droning on up there, I kept fantasizing about that Debbie Harry being up on stage instead. I've always fancied her.'

'Sexy,' groaned Alan.

'A good singer,' Phil agreed.

'I like her latest single,' Bobs-boy put in. 'I think it's "Call me". Otherwise, I'm not wild about her.'

'Well, she makes me detonate prematurely,' GG informed them. 'It's those lips.'

'The only detonation I'm looking forward to right now,' Inman said, 'is the one that's going to blow in the windows of that bleedin' Embassy. I want to get in there.'

'You just want to kill some terrorists,' said Jock, the Blue Team's staff-sergeant, who had just that moment entered the barracks to call the men out for more abseil training at Pearl House. 'Though I doubt if you'd mind if they were hostages, knowing you, Inman.'

'You wrong me,' Inman replied.

'*I* want to kill some terrorists,' Baby Face informed them all in his deceptively innocent, schoolboyish manner. 'I thought that's why we're here.'

'You're here to do as you're told,' said Sergeant Harrison, like Jock having just returned to barracks. He now stood beside his fellow team leader and said: 'And we're here to tell you to get off your backs and pack your kit for some abseiling. We move out in ten minutes.'

'It's better than nothing,' Inman said, swinging his legs off his camp-bed. 'Come on, men, let's go.'

In fact, if the demolition lectures were as boring as all the others, they did at least offer a slight respite. For the men, though not permitted to practice with real explosives within the confines of the Regent's Park Barracks, could at least tinker with defused explosive charges and detonators. This gave them something to do, other than listen to the droning voices of the 'green slime' or instructors from the Royal Signals, Royal Engineers, REME, RAMC, RAOC, and even the Hereford and Army School of Languages, whose representative had come to teach them some basic Arabic in case they needed to talk to the terrorists.

'I need to talk to a terrorist like I need a hole in the head,' Phil said in the back of the Avis van that was carrying them to Pimlico for another few hours of abseil training. 'If I hear any bastard talking in Arabic, I'll make sure it's his last words.'

'Most of the hostages speak Arabic,' Baby Face said in his quiet, solemn way, 'so that gives you a problem.'

'Not me, Trooper. I've no problem with that at all. My only interest is in saving the British hostages. To hell with the rest of them. So if any bastard speaks Arabic to me, he won't talk for much longer.'

'I second that,' Ken said firmly. 'Once we get in there, we won't have time to decide who's a terrorist and who's a hostage, so I say they either get down on the floor or they get their wings clipped. You tell them to shut up and lie down or you blow them to Kingdom Come. No two ways about it. If they insist on talking and the chat is in Arabic, I'm taking no chances. A short burst from the MP5 or a double tap; they'll get one or the other.'

'There's women in there as well,' Baby Face reminded them.

'Women terrorists?' Bobs-boy asked.

'No, hostages. Female hostages. I think all of them work in the Embassy and were there when the terrorists took it over. We can't shoot women, can we?'

'Why not?' Inman asked gruffly. 'Most married men want to shoot their wives, so we might be doing someone a favour if we stitch a few in the Embassy.'

'That's out of order,' Danny Boy said. 'Worse than picking on your dog instead of having it out with your neighbours.'

'How did neighbours and dogs get into this conversation?' Bobs-boy wanted to know.

'Never mind,' Danny Boy said.

In fact, he hated his neighbours. His home was on a grim Humberside council estate with his wife and two children, a boy and a girl, and he had been fighting with his neighbours for the past couple of years about his backyard fence, which they claimed clipped three inches off their own yard. Danny

Boy did not give a damn about his fence – he just could not stand the fat bastard, a butcher, who lived next door, so he continued the fight just for sport. While this amused him during his rare visits home, his wife Belinda, who let the kids run wild, was highly embarrassed, having once been best friends with her neighbour, Florence, the fat slob's wife. In truth, this knowledge only encouraged Danny Boy to keep up the aggro; it was his way of paying his slovenly wife back for letting the kids run wild, encouraged by that other slattern, Florence.

Yes, Danny Boy, who passionately loved his cat, Oscar, hated both his neighbours and had dreams of finding them cowering in the Embassy when finally he crashed in.

Not to stitch them, he thought. No, I wouldn't go that far. Just a couple of flash-bangs, followed by a dose of CS gas and an undiplomatic reception on the back lawn, face down in the grass and trussed up like chickens. That should teach them a lesson.

'I've got good neighbours,' said Ken, the Geordie. 'Where I come from, people are friendly and helpful, and so are the folks next door. We like to share a pint, get in some darts, have a night in the amusement arcade – all husbands and wives, like. It's a pretty good life.'

This was true enough. The only thing Ken missed when with the SAS was his life back in Newcastle upon Tyne, where the people – at least those still with a job – believed in working hard and playing hard without being too fancy.

Ken had had a job in a brickworks until he was eighteen, then he had met a girl from Keele, sweet-faced Beryl Williams, and discovered that she was as sweet as she looked, which is why she ended up pregnant, luckily by Ken. Doing the decent thing, he had married her and set up house in Keele, near his new wife's parents. They were as nice as she was, solid working-class, and had made terrific grandparents when the first child, Audrey, came along and was followed ten months later by Mel. By that time, Ken's wage from the brickworks was inadequate and he decided, in a spontaneous bid to better himself, to join the Army.

After his initial training, he was posted to the Staffordshire Regiment. Surprised to discover how much he enjoyed being away from home, but bored by life in the infantry, he had decided to try his luck with the SAS, which had already developed a glamorous reputation. Surprised again to get in, he had soon found himself in Oman, which was exactly the kind of exotic location he had joined the Regiment for. Unfortunately, he was only sent there in July 1976, and in September the SAS were pulled out of the country for good. By December that same year, he had found himself in Northern Ireland, which was considerably less exotic, though it certainly taught him a lot about CRW. Now, ironically, here he was again, about to fight a battle on British soil. You just couldn't credit it.

'The only good life you're going to find is right here with the Regiment,' his good friend and fellow trooper, Alan Pyle, told him. 'You'd be worthless without it. Working in a brickworks, for God's sakes. Who wants to know about *that?*'

'Oh, I had a good time,' Ken replied distractedly, thinking about his many good times. 'It wasn't that bad, really.'

'Sounds bloody boring to me, but one man's meat . . .'

Alan had his own idea of a good time, which was going to the dogs, spending a few bob in the bookies, having a night out with the boys, or shagging his arse off. Born to decent, middle-class parents, both teachers, in Swiss Cottage, north London, and educated in private schools, including the London School of Economics, Alan had rebelled at seventeen.

Having taken to drink and drugs, he dropped out of the LSE and slipped into a dreamy kind of non-existence in a sordid shared flat in Notting Hill Gate. In just such a state, he had attended an army recruiting drive for a laugh. To his amazement, when his mind was straight again, he found that he had been accepted and was in for the full term.

No longer on drugs, though with an abiding fondness for drink, he had relished the singular disciplines of life in the 2nd Battalion, Queen's Regiment, but often found himself yearning for something more. Desperate to get away when he got a WRAC corporal pregnant during a night of sin after a drink-sodden party, he had been persuaded by a close and similarly compromised friend to apply for the SAS.

Accepted and badged, Alan had been posted straight to Northern Ireland and found, once again to his amazement, that he loved it because it was dangerous. Still single and not desperate to be married, he had thrown himself whole-heartedly into the disciplines of the Regiment, as well as into its unique social world. Since much of that world was centred around the Sports and Social Club in Hereford, he became firm friends not only with his fellow troopers, but with NCOs such as Lance-Corporal Phil McArthur and Corporal George Gerrard, both veterans of Oman and Northern Ireland, both bachelors and both good fun. Though Alan was still basically an educated, middle-class Londoner slightly removed from the other troopers, he felt at ease with men older and more experienced than himself – veterans like Phil and GG. Such men were amused by Alan's drawled, sardonic comments and treated him kindly. They were also pleased that he genuinely respected them and did not try to put them down.

'I joined the army to see the world,' Ken said, 'and here I am in the back of an Avis van, seeing only the West End.'

'But you'll soon be high above it all,' Alan reminded him, 'so appreciate what you've got.'

'What I've got is a sore arse from sitting on those hard chairs in that freezing lecture hall. I can't pretend it's a hoot.'

'You'll come to life when you get up on that roof and do some abseiling,' Inman assured him. 'We'll all wake up then.'

'At least it's something to do,' said Baby Face.

He was right, for although the lessons in demolition gave them a reason to use at least their hands, tinkering with explosive charges and detonators, they failed to offer a way of letting off steam or getting rid of excess energy. Abseiling, on the other hand, was as near as they would get to adventurous physical activity while in the holding area of the Regent's Park Barracks. Originating in Malaya as an SAS Standard Operating Procedure (SOP) used to let a soldier make a quick descent from a helicopter with the aid of a rope and harness, it was being practised rigorously by each man. It provided a means of gaining access to the various balconies of the 80-foot-high Embassy, by lowering themselves down the sides and rear of the building. For this reason, nylon abseiling ropes had secretly been tied to the chimneys of the Embassy during the first day of the siege and were still coiled up there on the roof, ready for the arrival of the SAS abseilers.

At Pearl House, which was almost as high as the Iranian Embassy, the men spent nearly all day on the windswept roof, taking apart and reassembling the abseiling equipment, then lowering themselves as rapidly as possible down the back wall, using a system considered too dangerous by even skilled mountaineers because there are many ways in which it can go wrong.

The abseiling equipment consisted of a strong nylon rope, a harness and a metal device, the descendeur, which was clipped to the harness and through which the rope was then threaded. Manipulation of the descendeur against the rope as the abseiler drops creates a 'friction break', enabling the wearer to control his rate of descent: slow, medium or rapid.

Though favoured by the SAS because of its convenience and speed during an assault, abseiling is in fact a highly dangerous activity that has caused many deaths among climbers, novices and veterans alike, even in non-combat situations.

Nevertheless, abseil training remained one of the few activities that allowed the men to let off excess energy when they were stood down yet again and returned from the FHA at the Royal College of Medical Practitioners to the holding area in Regent's Park Barracks. Besides, abseiling was dangerous and most of the men had joined the SAS partly because they got a kick out of taking risks.

Unfortunately, the abseil training was usually followed either by another 'Hyde Park' signal calling them out on stand-by and another frustrating stand-down, or by more hours of mind-numbing lectures about subjects they had already covered time and time again.

This particular day, Day Three of the siege, after the men had repeatedly gone over the edge of the roof of Pearl House and dropped down the side of the building – sometimes all the way to the ground; at other times stopping and entering the building via balcony windows; all the time observed and applauded by admiring police constables and officers – they were driven back to their temporary barracks and allowed to get the only good night's sleep they would have for a long time.

They were called out of bed first thing in the morning by yet another 'Hyde Park' alert.

9

Day Four began with a conversation between Salim and the police on the field telephone, during which the former poured out his frustrations at the lack of progress in negotiations and insisted that because of 'British deceit' the British hostages would now be the last to be freed. Again he insisted on speaking once more to the BBC and when again this was refused, he said that a hostage would have to die.

The police knew that inside the Embassy, as one terrorist stood guard over the hostages, trying to stay awake, the others, distracted by the sound of drilling as more probes and bugs were inserted in the walls, were prowling restlessly, guns lifted, expecting an attack through wall or ceiling at any time.

On the roof, the members of the SAS's Red Team were quietly checking that their ropes were still in position. Satisfied, they tiptoed away, clambered onto the adjoining college's roof, then made their way back down to the FHA, where the mood was increasingly tense.

'He's run his string out to the limit,' Sergeant Inman said, 'and it's going to break any minute now.'

'Then his kite flies away,' Baby Face said with a faint but deadly smile. 'We won't have too long to wait.'

'Dead right,' Inman said.

The demands and offers were repeated throughout the day as the police played a cat-and-mouse game with the terrorists. Because they knew that the terrorists would be listening to the news on the radio, they called a press conference at which they avoided the word 'terrorist' and referred instead to 'hostage takers'. Eventually, however, Salim's threat to kill a hostage compelled them to bring a BBC news desk deputy editor, Tony Crabb, to the Embassy to talk to the terrorist leader.

Speaking from an upstairs window on behalf of the latter, one of the BBC hostages, Sim Harris, asked Crabb why he had not broadcast Salim's statements. When Crabb blandly replied that there had been a 'misunderstanding', Harris replied: 'You must put out the right statement; otherwise everyone here could be killed.'

Before Crabb could reply, two other hostages, PC Lock and the Syrian journalist, Mustafa Karkouti, appeared at the window to tell Crabb and the police negotiator that Salim was in deadly earnest about his threat to start the killing.

'All right,' the negotiator finally said. 'I'll personally take down Salim's statement and make sure it's correct.'

When the negotiator had taken out his notebook and pen and was ready to take down what Salim said, the latter, standing behind Mustafa Karkouti and aiming a pistol at his head, relayed his statement through the Syrian. Talking from the shadows behind Karkouti, he repeated his personal details, then made his statement, which the police officer carefully wrote down, word for word.

'One: We swear to God and to the British people and Government that no danger whatsoever will be inflicted on the British and non-Iranian hostages if the British Government and the British police don't kid the group and don't subject the life of the hostages and the group to any danger, and if things work to the contradictory direction everyone in the building will be harmed.

'Two: We demand the three ambassadors Algerian, Jordanian and Iraqi – and a representative of the Red Cross to start their jobs in negotiating between us and the British Government to secure the safety of the hostages as well as the group's members and to terminate the whole operation peacefully. If any of the three ambassadors is not available he could be substituted by first the Libyan, or the Syrian or the Kuwait ambassador.

'Three: The reason for us to come to Britain to carry out this operation is because of the pressure and oppression which is being practised by the Iranian Government in Arabistan and to convey our voice to the outside world through your country. Once again, we apologize to the people and the Government for this inconvenience.'

Salim stepped out of the shadows to peer over Karkouti's shoulder and check that the negotiator was writing everything down. When the officer stopped writing and glanced up from his notebook, Salim added, through Karkouti: 'And I demand a guarantee that this time my statement will be broadcast accurately and as soon as possible.'

'OK,' the negotiator replied. 'But what do we get in return?'

Salim thought about this for a moment, then replied: 'What do you want?'

'The release of some hostages.'

'One,' Salim said.

'More than one,' the negotiator said. 'How about three?'

'Two,' Salim said.

The police officer nodded. 'Agreed.' There was silence for a long time, then the negotiator asked: 'Who will be released.'

'One moment. We must decide,' Salim said, then both men disappeared from the window. A considerable period of time passed before the two men returned, with Salim still aiming his pistol at Karkouti's head.

'Two,' he said. 'Haideh Kanji and Ali-Ghola Ghanzanfar.'

Another police officer, who had come up to stand beside the negotiator, now flipped through his notebook, studied a list of names, then said: 'Kanji's the twenty-three-year-old secretary to the Embassy's two accountants. Being three months pregnant, she's an obvious choice.'

'And Ghanzanfar?'

'A Pakistani educationalist. According to the statement of a previously released hostage, he snores dreadfully at night – so loud that he even annoyed the terrorists. They're probably glad to get rid of him.'

The negotiator grinned. 'I suppose so. Well, it's better than nothing.' Again using the radio phone, he asked Salim if the hostages were to be released before or after the promised BBC broadcast.

'After,' Salim said.

'We want them before.'

'No. They are my safeguard that the broadcast will be made and done correctly – on the nine o'clock news.'

'Release one before and one after,' the negotiator suggested patiently.

'No. Both hostages will be released immediately after the broadcast.'

'Then *we* have no guarantee. We could make the broadcast and you could then break your word and keep the hostages.'

Salim exploded with fury behind Karkouti. 'I do not break my word!' he screamed.

'What if we refuse to make the broadcast unless the two hostages are released first?' the negotiator asked calmly when Salim had calmed down.

'If my statement is not read at nine tonight,' Salim replied, 'I'll kill a hostage and send out the body.'

Hearing that statement, Karkouti sank to his knees in full view of everyone, obviously pleading with Salim not to do anything rash. PC Lock appeared just behind him, framed by the window, to lean down and whisper comforting words to him.

Surprisingly, Salim then screamed in frustration at PC Lock, his words carrying clearly to the police officers in the middle of the road. 'What can we do? We treat you well, we like you, we agree with what you say, but the police do not keep their word!' He then grabbed Karkouti by the shoulder, jerked him upright, and pushed him and PC Lock out of sight.

'Well, do we make the broadcast or not?' Crabb, the BBC news desk deputy editor, asked the police officers. The one standing beside the negotiator nodded. 'Yes.' He held his hand out to the negotiator. The latter tore Salim's statement from his notebook and passed it over. 'Let's go back to my trailer,' the senior police officer said, 'and I'll give you a photocopy of this statement. Then you can take yourself off to Broadcasting House and arrange for it to be read out on the nine o'clock news, unless you receive a message stating otherwise. You stay here,' he said to the negotiator, 'and keep him engaged.'

'Will do,' the negotiator said, glancing up at the window as the other two departed. There was no one at the window. Indeed, no one returned for a long time, which enabled the negotiator to leave for lunch. When he returned, there was still no one at the window. He kept leaving and returning until, when he was in one of the police trailers, sharing a cup of tea with some fellow officers, another message came through on the field telephone, informing him that Salim wished to speak to him. Hurrying to the front of the Embassy, the negotiator waited patiently and eventually, at just before six p.m., Salim appeared at the window, standing as usual behind the now frightened Karkouti.

'On the advice of my friends,' Salim said through the Syrian, 'I have decided to show good faith by releasing the woman hostage before the broadcast is made tonight. She is coming out now.'

While Salim was speaking, the front door of the Embassy opened and the face of a terrorist wearing a *keffia* peered around it. Satisfied that no one was attempting to charge the building, he opened the door and stepped aside to let the pregnant woman, Haideh Kanji, leave the building. She did so slowly, carefully, as if not quite believing what was happening, then walked more quickly once she had stepped off the pavement and was on the road. The terrorist slammed the door shut just before the hostage reached the negotiator. The woman was weeping for joy. Up on the scaffolding of the press enclosure, photographers with telephoto lenses were frantically taking pictures.

The negotiator took Haideh Kanji by the arm and started leading her towards the police barricades, but before they had reached them two medics hurried from the throng to help her the rest of the way. When all three had disappeared back into the crowd packed along the barricade, the negotiator turned back to face the Embassy window. Using his field telephone, he thanked Salim for releasing the woman and assured him that his statement would be broadcast that evening.

Three hours later, on the nine o'clock news, Deputy Assistant Commissioner Peter Neivens, the head of information at Scotland Yard, meticulously read out Salim's statement.

Within minutes of that broadcast, the second hostage, Ali-Ghola Ghanzanfar, was released from the Embassy.

10

'According to the released hostage, Ali-Ghola,' the Controller of the SAS CQB team said to the other members of COBR at a meeting in the evening of Day Five, 'everyone in the Embassy, including the hostages, was overjoyed at hearing Salim's statement broadcast. They cried, hugged and kissed each other. Even the terrorists cried – at least, all except Salim. They were also jubilant when the two hostages were released. Indeed, as Ghanzanfar was being led away from the other hostages, to leave the building for good, the remaining terrorists joined the hostages in their room, sitting with them, their guns in their laps, all laughing and joking together. By way of celebration, and as a conciliatory gesture, the police then sent in a dinner ordered from Pars, a nearby Persian restaurant. So a good time, as best we know, was had by terrorists and hostages alike.'

'I think the celebratory meal was a touch of genius,' the Secretary said. 'It must have lowered the temperature considerably and brought the terrorists and hostages closer together, at least temporarily.'

'Naturally, I agree,' the Police Commissioner said.

'You would,' the Controller said with a grin, before glancing down at his notes and growing serious again. 'Anyway, to get back to the real business, we have a problem with this demand linking the release of hostages to some sort of intervention by the ambassadors. In my view, there's no serious hope that the negotiators can deliver a deal on that hypothesis.'

'You're correct in that assessment,' the genial Secretary said. 'The Foreign Office has already been on the phone to the Kuwaiti Ambassador, Sheik Saud Nasir Al-Sabah, and the Jordanian chargé d'affaires, Kasim Ghazzawi. So far, while both men expressed their willingness to discuss the matter at a later date, neither has showed willingness to help or involve themselves in the matter unless we offer safe conduct for the terrorists. As that's something we simply cannot do, the talks ended in deadlock.'

'What about the International Committee of the Red Cross?' the Commissioner asked.

'Earlier this afternoon they announced that, provided all parties were agreeable, they would send their delegates into the Embassy to give first-aid treatment, if necessary, and to assist communications between all parties concerned. While their motives are no doubt humane, their mention of first-aid treatment and material and moral comfort has merely added to the increasingly doom-laden atmosphere.'

'Does Salim know about this?'

'Not exactly – though he must surely suspect it. Certainly, just before this meeting convened, he reduced his demands again. Now he wants only one ambassador to mediate, and a guarantee of safe passage for him and his comrades.'

'He is, however, close to the edge,' the Controller reminded them. 'Which means he's unpredictable.'

'Nevertheless,' the Commissioner insisted, 'we have to keep talking at all costs in the hope of averting an attack on the Embassy in which the hostages might be killed along with the terrorists.'

'I'm not trying to push for my men,' the Controller said. 'I'm just not sure that all this talking is getting us anywhere.'

'I should point out to you,' the Commissioner countered, 'that our record for handling siege situations has so far been impeccable. There have been two similar sieges in recent times. The first was at the Spaghetti House restaurant in Knightsbridge in October 1975, when three gunmen barricaded themselves in a basement with six waiters. In the second, two months later, four IRA terrorists seized a married couple in their council flat in Balcombe Street, Marylebone, holding them hostage for six days and nights. Both situations presented the Metropolitan Police with highly sensitive issues on the ground, as well as possible international repercussions depending upon the outcome. In both cases our tactics brought the siege to a successful conclusion, with the hostages released unharmed and the gunmen surrendering.'

'I'm not arguing with your tactics,' insisted the Controller. 'I'm only worried that the constant talking and general indecision is placing a strain on my men – as, indeed, it's already doing with the police.'

'If you're referring to the fact that the strain has led to one of my men being replaced, I should point out that so far he's the only one, which is really not that high a price to pay.'

'It's not its effect on our own men,' the Controller said. 'We also have to take into account the effect it may be having on the terrorists. It is my belief, for instance, that their leader, Salim, is getting close to the edge. As we all know, thanks to the audio-surveillance devices implanted in the walls of the building, the tension did explode earlier this morning over something quite trivial. That row led to yet another false alert for my two assault teams.'

The SAS man was referring to a row that erupted when some of the terrorists sprayed subversive slogans on the walls of a room where the hostages were kept. The chargé d'affaires, Dr Afrouz, had been incensed by the slogans and strongly voiced his opinion to the terrorists involved. Even more incensed, however, was another hostage, Abbas Lavasani. Being the most devout member of the Embassy staff, Lavasani was furious at the written insults against Ayatollah Khomeini and engaged in an argument with those responsible. One of the terrorists angrily pulled out his gun and was only prevented from shooting Lavasani by the diplomatic intervention of the Muslim journalist Muhammad Farughi. PC Lock and Karkouti then hurried Lavasani out of the room where, out of earshot of the angry terrorists, Karkouti reprimanded him for letting his temper spoil all the gains of the past two days. When the Syrian also told Lavasani that he, as a man of God, should not let himself be responsible for the deaths of the other hostages, Lavasani burst into tears.

'That row,' the Controller said, 'was an indication that both terrorists and hostages are becoming more volatile. A lot could develop out of that – and none of it good.'

'Nevertheless,' the Commissioner said, 'I insist that we keep playing for time. The longer the siege can be maintained, the greater the chances of getting the hostages out alive. A lengthy siege also presents the distinct possibility of psychological transference, in which the individuals, terrorist and hostage alike, develop sympathy for one another and even, in certain cases, become friends. If such a situation develops – and it certainly has in the past – the terrorists will be more likely to release their hostages. Failing that, we can at least reach a situation where we can convince the terrorists that they cannot get away and it would be in their own interests to come out peacefully. It is my belief that as Salim has already decided against blowing up the building, and has since reduced his demands, there is a chance that he will indeed decide that he has gained what he most wanted – publicity for his cause – and therefore needs to take it no further. In other words, he might yet come out without a fight.'

'He won't come out peacefully if we deny him safe passage out of the country – and we all know that's something we cannot agree to. Sooner or later that knowledge will sink in . . . then what will he do?'

Mercifully the ensuing silence was broken by the shrill ringing of the red telephone on the Secretary's desk. Picking it up, he listened thoughtfully. Then he smiled and put the receiver down again.

'Some good news at last,' he said. 'Apparently the Syrian journalist, Mustafa Karkouti, has been suffering from severe diarrhoea and fever. For that reason Salim has just released him. He's presently being debriefed in a Metropolitan Police HQ trailer outside the Embassy, so I suggest you both take yourselves over there and hear what he has to say.'

'Damned right,' the Controller said.

Leaving the basement room, they took the lift up to the ground floor and left the building by the guarded front doors. A chauffeur-driven limousine was waiting for them outside in the lamplit darkness of Whitehall. Once in the car, they were driven quickly to Kensington, making small talk about the siege until they arrived at the police barricades in Princes Gate. As he clambered out of the limousine, the Controller glanced up to see the great canvas marquee of the press enclosure in Hyde Park. There, high up on the floodlit scaffolding, dozens of photographers were perched like black birds, cameras at the ready. 'At least they've got a head for heights,' the Controller said as he hurried beside the Commissioner to the trailer being used as the police HQ, pushing his way through milling ambulance men. Identified by the constable on guard outside the trailer, he let the Commissioner enter first, then followed him up the three steps and through the open door.

Inside, an exhausted, ill-looking Mustafa Karkouti was sitting in a hard wooden chair, virtually surrounded by men from the Metropolitan Police intelligence department, as well as one white-smocked medic. The latter had just removed a thermometer from Karkouti's mouth and was thoughtfully studying it. As the Police Commissioner introduced the SAS Controller to those who did not know him, the medic grinned at Karkouti and said: 'Those tablets are working. Your temperature's dropped to normal already and your blood pressure's OK. When these men have finished with you, we'll take you to the hospital for no more than a good rest and observation. After that, you'll be all right.'

'Thank you,' Karkouti said with a slight smile of relief, as the medic packed up his little bag and left the long, packed trailer.

'Has he given you much so far?' the Commissioner whispered to one of his senior police officers.

'A windfall,' came the whispered reply. 'We know everything that's going on inside: the names, the weapons, the whereabouts of the hostages, the psychological state of the terrorists. He sent out the wrong hostage.'

'Wrong for him, right for us,' the Commissioner noted.

'Correct.'

'Has he finished talking?'

'No. He's just about to tell us what's happened since Ghanzanfar was released. He believes that Salim's authority over the rest of the team – uneducated men in their twenties – is fading because the siege is going on too long. They were told it would last no longer than twenty-four hours, so now they're pretty unhappy.'

The Commissioner nodded and glanced at the Controller, then both of them sat at the back of the trailer, in the shadows well away from Karkouti and those talking to him.

'So the last time you saw them in good mood was when Ali-Ghola Ghanzanfar was released?' the police interrogator asked.

'Yes,' the journalist replied. 'We all had such a good time together when Ghanzanfar was released, sharing that Persian meal sent in by the police – rice, kebabs and Bandit biscuits, washed down with Tango orange and Pepsi. Ron Morris used an orange crate as a table. He even put paper napkins on it. PC Lock and Morris had a cheerful conversation, the latter swearing that once released, he would never go back to working in the Embassy, the former insisting that he would return because he liked the work so much.'

'I know PC Lock,' the interrogator said, trying to make the conversation as casual as possible. 'He's a constable who loves his work, so he'll go back to work.'

Karkouti smiled. 'I suppose we *all* will.'

'So for a time there, when you were having that meal, you were almost like friends.'

'Yes. In fact, the atmosphere was so euphoric, Salim even gave me an interview. I'd been trying to get one since the start of the siege and he finally relented. He just sat there with his rifle across his lap, smiling – as he normally never did – and talking his head off.'

'You took notes?'

'Of course.' Karkouti handed over his notebook. The interrogator scanned it quickly. 'It's lengthy and detailed,' he said, 'so I'll only summarize it. When we're done here, I'll have the notes photocopied and give you all copies.' He paused as he went back to the start of the notes, then he said: 'It confirms that Salim is twenty-seven years old, comes from a middle-class family, studied at Tehran University, graduated from the Linguistics Faculty, participated in the Iranian students' struggle, and was indeed imprisoned and tortured by SAVAK. His occupation of the Embassy he views as self-defence, meaning resistance to what he calls the Ayatollah's cruel Farsi-ization of the Arabistan province and his relentless exploitation of Iranian Arabs. His aim is to help gain autonomy for his people in Arabistan and regain the name 'Arabistan' instead of its present name, 'Khuzistan'. The purpose of the Embassy take-over is to gain publicity for his cause and place pressure on the Iranian Government through world public opinion. He hopes that the take-over will end peacefully, though this depends entirely on the British authorities and the Arab ambassadors whom he'd asked to be brought here.' Lowering the notebook to his lap, the interrogator said to Karkouti: 'This information will be invaluable in shedding light on their behaviour and possible actions.'

'Good,' Karkouti said.

'So what happened after the meal?'

'We were taken down to the Ambassador's room on the first floor, where we had the best sleep we'd had since the siege commenced. I think we all slept soundly because we took the broadcast and release of the other hostages as hopeful signs.'

'What about the following morning? This morning.'

'The mood was still euphoric. The terrorists heard the early news bulletins claiming that the Arab ambassadors were willing to help.'

'Which was wrong,' the interrogator said.

'None of us were to know that,' Karkouti said. 'We all thought they were true.'

'Sorry. Please continue.'

'The untrue stories about the Arab ambassadors, combined with the news that the Red Cross were standing by, naturally filled Salim and his fellow gunmen with optimism. Being in good mood, they ran a bath and offered to let us use it first. PC Lock and I were the first to receive invitations. I said, quite rightly, that it would be discourteous to bathe in front of the woman, but PC Lock said he wanted to keep his uniform on to preserve his image.'

'His *image?*'

Karkouti smiled tiredly. 'That's what he said. His real purpose was to ensure that the terrorists did not find the pistol strapped to his thigh.'

'A clever man, PC Lock.'

Karkouti nodded. 'Yes. Anyway, as the deadline passed, boredom set in again and the terrorists – who were now also complaining about how long they had been in the Embassy – tried to distract themselves by scrawling subversive slogans on the walls of our room with magic marker pens.'

'Exactly what did the slogans say?'

'"Long live the Arabistani people." "We demand fundamental changes." "Death to Khomeini" . . . and so on. Salim had to ask the Muslim journalist Muhammad Farughi how to spell "fundamental".'

'From what we picked up from our audio-surveillance devices, Farughi kept a low profile regarding this.'

'Yes. He was taking down notes for an article he hoped to write some day. He copied down the slogans on the wall even as the gunmen were writing them.'

'Then the row began with Dr Afrouz and Abbas Lavasani.'

'You heard all that through your bugging devices?' Karkouti asked.

'Yes.'

Karkouti shook his head in wonderment. 'That is truly amazing.'

'What about after the row was over? Do you think it had an effect on the relationship between the terrorists and the hostages?'

'Yes. Definitely. We had been growing closer together, more considerate of each other, but all that ended with the row over the slogans. Now, they were distant to us again. Also, it was clear that they'd had enough and just wanted out. They complained to Salim about it. They said the police would not take them seriously unless they killed someone. That's when Salim reduced his demands again by settling for one Arab ambassador and asking only for a guarantee of safe passage for him and his men. Salim was now very tired and, I think, disillusioned. Like his men, he just wanted out, but he had his pride to protect.'

'And, shortly after reducing his demand, he decided to let you go?'

'Yes. By now, my diarrhoea and fever had been followed by a numbness in the arms and legs and I found it painful to urinate. Even so, when he made the offer, I asked him to let one of the women go instead of me. He refused, insisting that I needed medical attention. Then he walked me downstairs to the front door and once there, let me out.'

'Did you have any final words together?'

'Yes. He confessed that he was depressed because the operation had been planned to last for about twenty-four hours and now it had gone on for nearly a week.'

'Anything else?'

Karkouti took a deep breath, then let it out slowly. 'He said I was to tell you that if you didn't get in touch with the Arab ambassadors something bad would happen.'

'Those were his exact words?'

'Yes. He said . . . "something bad".'

Hearing these words, the SAS Controller stood up and hurried out of the trailer, determined to talk to his men and prepare them for action.

11

The sixth day found the Red and Blue Teams still practising their abseiling techniques in Pimlico. Recalled to the FHA at the Royal College of Medical Practitioners, they were informed by the Controller that the Home Secretary had turned the screws on the terrorists again by letting them know that the 'ambassadorial' phase had passed and that the only concession they would get was a visit from an imam from the Regent's Park Mosque.

'The Home Secretary's hoping that the Iman will act as a mediator,' the Controller said, 'but whether he does or not, I think the killing will start eventually. If it does, the Deliberate Assault Plan will require two hours' notice to succeed. This plan's the one that gives the maximum chance of surprise and best hope of hostage survival. The not-so-good news is that even if all goes as intended, the best chance of saving hostage life is no more than sixty per cent of the total.'

'So what if we have more time, boss?' Red Team's Lance-Corporal Phil McArthur asked. 'What, for instance, if we get another full day's preparation and training?'

'I'd estimate that by then both plans – Immediate Action and Deliberate Assault – would merge into a response time of a few minutes.'

'Then maybe we should all say our prayers that the talking's continuing,' Blue Team's Corporal George Gerrard said.

'Maybe,' the Controller said. 'The only problem with that is that suddenly time seems to be running out. According to a message from PC Lock, Salim's self-control finally snapped this morning. First, he told Lock that he thought the police were drilling through the walls to try to get into the building. In fact, they were drilling holes for the insertion of fibre-optic and spike cameras. This led to the plaster on the first-floor landing bulging out.'

'Dumb bastards,' Sergeant Inman said.

'Salim saw the bulging wall and went mad. Luckily, PC Lock managed to convince him that even if the police *were* intending to break through the walls and storm the building, they would certainly not do it during the day, but only at night.'

'Lock's response was clever,' Danny Boy said. 'He bought some more time.'

'Unfortunately, it didn't end there,' the Controller continued.

'I don't think I can listen to any more of this,' Bobs-boy whispered to his fellow trooper, Baby Face.

'Given the sparseness of sockets for their bugs, the police simply lowered them from the roof down the chimneys. As they should have known would happen, bits of debris were dislodged by the bugs and made a lot of noise when they fell. Salim went mad again.'

'I don't bloody believe it!' Jock Thompson spluttered. 'It's us, not the police, who should be planting the surveillance devices. If we did, at least the job would be done properly and not cocked up every inch of the way. What a bloody waste!'

'Even worse,' the Controller continued remorselessly, 'Iran's Foreign Minister sent the *hostages* a telegram, praising them for their forbearance in the face of the quote, "criminal actions",

114

unquote, of Ba'athist Iraq. He also informed the hostages that Iran would spare no effort for their release and that thousands of Iranians were ready to enter the Embassy to bring punishment to the mercenaries, meaning the terrorists. Naturally, Salim read the telegram and was further incensed.'

'Poor boy!' Staff-Sergeant Harrison exclaimed sardonically. 'Nobody loves him.'

'Finally, finding all this too much to take, Salim exploded and told Lock to inform the police that unless there was a prompt answer to his demand for the ambassadors to come into the negotiations, a hostage would be shot in half an hour. He then moved the male hostages out of the large second-floor room where they had been for days and took them down the hall to the telex room – Room 10 – overlooking Princes Gate.

'And the women?' Trooper Ken Passmore asked.

'They're still where they were, in Room 9A, overlooking the rear gardens.'

'Any other changes in atmosphere since that move?' Sergeant Inman asked.

'Well, both PC Lock and Sim Harris have made it clear by phone and, after that, through a conversation between them and Police Superintendent Fred Luff – conducted on the part of Lock and Harris from the first-floor front balcony – that they're alarmed at the changed atmosphere. So much so, in fact, that they warned Luff that they feel they're in danger. They started sensing this when the terrorists put on their anoraks and wound their *keffias* tightly around their heads. That means they're ready to fight or kill.'

'Were Lock and Harris given any message to take back to the terrorists?' Harrison asked.

'Yes. They were told to tell Salim that the Foreign Office was still holding discussions with the designated ambassadors and that if he listened to the BBC World Service's midday news bulletin, he would hear confirmation of that fact.'

'*I* listened to that news bulletin,' Inman said, 'and I heard sweet FA.'

'Exactly,' the Controller responded. 'That's why the trouble will start soon. In fact, Salim has given us forty-five minutes before he kills the first hostage.'

That turned out to be the case. Abbas Lavasani, a deeply devout, unmarried twenty-eight-year-old, had arrived only two weeks before to take up his position as the Embassy's chief press officer. A phone call that afternoon from PC Lock to the police negotiator revealed that Lavasani had volunteered to be a martyr after the bitter row with Salim about the terrorist leader's anti-Khomeini graffiti.

Subsequently, at one-thirty, only a few hours after the SAS Controller's briefing with his men, when Lavasani indicated that he wished to visit the lavatory, Salim led him out of the telex room where the male hostages were held and down to the ground floor. There, after letting Lavasani use the lavatory, Salim had argued with the police over the radio telephone. He then handed the phone to PC Lock, who was present with Sim Harris, and told him to inform the police negotiators that he had a man whom he was going to shoot. While Lock was doing so, Salim ordered two of the other terrorists to truss Lavasani's hands behind his back and then tie him to the bottom of the banisters. He made Lock inform the negotiators of this fact also.

When Lock had described the chilling details of this scene, the negotiators, still playing for time, said the ambassadors would meet at five p.m. When Lock had passed this message on to Salim, he and Sim Harris were conducted back upstairs to rejoin the other hostages in the telex room.

Shortly afterwards, they heard Lavasani talking on the telephone, identifying himself to the police negotiators outside. Even as he uttered his own name, he was cut off by Salim's: 'No names! No names!' Then there were three shots in quick succession. Some hostages thought they heard groaning, others a choking sound. Silence followed.

Salim finally broke that silence by speaking himself to the negotiators on the phone, telling them that he had just killed a man.

According to PC Lock's subsequent phone conversation with the negotiators, Salim, looking pale, then entered the telex room to tell the hostages that he had shot Lavasani.

'If you've killed a hostage then your cause is finished,' Ron Morris told him. You can kill all of us now. One or twenty makes no difference. Your cause is lost.'

'I am prepared to die,' Salim told him, then walked out of the telex room.

12

Most of those outside the Embassy could not believe that the killing had started. There was no sign of a body and the possibility remained that Salim was bluffing.

One of the few who contradicted this view, however, was the Controller, who insisted that the time was right for such an event and that a hostage had almost certainly been killed.

An hour after Salim's announcement, COBR was again in session in its basement room in Whitehall. There, while glancing at the television set flickering in one corner, waiting for the news, the Secretary, no longer quite so amiable, said: 'I *do* believe that until we receive proof that a hostage is dead it would be disastrous to react as if we believe it actually happened.'

'It happened,' the Controller insisted.

'Shots were heard,' the Police Commissioner said. 'Salim said he had killed a hostage. That doesn't constitute proof. Salim *could* be bluffing.'

'Whether he's bluffing or not,' the Secretary said, 'he's accepted the five o'clock deadline for a meeting with the Arab ambassadors, none of whom are likely to show up without the promise of safe conduct for the terrorists. If that happens, we'll have to pass control of the situation from the police to the SAS.'

'I can't argue with that,' the Commissioner said. 'We have no other option.'

'My thanks,' the Controller said.

'Not at all,' the Commissioner replied. 'No point in playing brinkmanship in a situation like this.'

'Very sporting,' the Controller said.

'We're a nation that loves sport.'

'So what happens,' the Secretary said, not amused by their banter, but turning his attention to the Controller, 'when that deadline arrives without sight of the ambassadors? Or, heaven forbid, when the terrorists produce proof of murder?'

'Our preparations for a Deliberate Attack will be completed by that time. From five p.m. onwards the assault can be launched with minimum delay. I should point out, however, that my men will have a better chance of success if they're given the go-ahead before nightfall – at eight-thirty.'

'Agreed,' the Commissioner said.

'What's vital, even imperative, is that between the time proof of murder is produced and the start of our assault, the terrorists should be fed a cover story to keep them happy and off guard.'

'I think you can depend on my negotiators to do that,' the Commissioner replied. 'They've been doing it for six days, after all, and made no mistakes so far.'

'I have one other point to make,' the Controller said. 'It's that the soldiers, once committed, should be left to get on with their job. If the Deliberate Assault is approved then halted at the last moment, it would be a disaster for morale.'

This did not sit too well with the Secretary who, in the manner of such men, wished to steer a careful middle course.

'I would,' he said, 'like to keep the emergency cover in place. This still allows the police to pass control to the SAS at short notice if multiple murders start inside the Embassy.'

'And if they don't?' the Controller asked testily.

'I'm not sure about that yet. Before making a decision, I'd like to take further counsel with the Police Commissioner here. I would also wish to inform both the Prime Minister and the Defence Minister at what might be termed the moment of decision. For now, other imponderables remain, such as: Is there a body?'

'I say no,' the Commissioner said.

'I say yes,' the Controller said.

'Why can't we just demand proof of Salim's claim by asking to see the corpse?'

'Because if we did,' the Commissioner said, 'and he hasn't yet actually killed someone, he might do so just to furnish us with proof.'

'Ah!' the Secretary said, still easily surprised, even in his mature years, by the slippery nature of politics.

'So what about the Arab ambassadors, due to show up at the Embassy at five?'

'I don't believe they'll show up,' the Controller said. 'According to my intelligence, they're gathered together right now at the offices of the Arab League in Green Street, Mayfair, trying to resolve their confusion over their supposed role in the whole business. They're particularly aggrieved because they believe that the Foreign Office has deliberately spread the notion that the initiative in all dealings with the terrorists has been taken by the Arabs, not by the FO.'

'Are they right?' the Commissioner asked.

'Of course,' the Secretary said with a bland smile. 'But don't say I told you so.'

'Anyway, there's little doubt,' the Controller continued, 'that the Arab ambassadors, while expressing their overriding concern to save life, will avoid all involvement by insisting on a safe passage out. They know we can't give them that.'

'But what if they do decide to take part?' the cautious Secretary asked. 'Whose terms do we play by? Ours or theirs?'

'Ours,' the Commissioner said. 'This is happening on the streets of London. I want them to turn up in good time or, failing that, I want clear guarantees that they *will* be coming. I don't want any failed promises based on our supposed guarantee of safe passage for the terrorists. They either come on our terms or not at all.'

'I think not at all,' the Controller said sardonically, 'because they won't want involvement unless they can arrange that safe passage. That would protect them from criticism. Those men have their own motives.'

'Why don't we avoid the ambassadors altogether,' the Secretary asked, 'by simply calling Salim's bluff and letting the deadline pass?'

'Because if no one has been killed so far,' the Commissioner replied, 'and I do not believe they have, then calling Salim's bluff could actually lead to the first killing. The blame would then fall squarely on us.'

The Secretary sighed and glanced at his watch. 'Four-forty-five,' he said. 'Fifteen minutes to go. Let's have a drink, gentlemen, and see if the Arab ambassadors show up.'

'Not a hope,' the Controller said.

Fifteen minutes later, at exactly five p.m., with the television news showing no new developments outside the Embassy, the Commissioner phoned his on-the-ground trailer HQ to enquire if anything had happened. Putting the phone down again, he glanced at the Controller, then turned reluctantly to the Secretary. 'My friend here was right,' he said graciously. 'None of the ambassadors showed up.'

The Secretary spread his hands on the table and lightly drummed his fingers. After pursing his lips, as if tasting a vintage wine, he asked: 'And what about the terrorists? Have they responded at all?'

'Not so far,' the Commissioner replied.

The Secretary glanced at his watch again. 'One minute past the deadline,' he said. 'Let's give them time to think about it and see what transpires. Another drink, gentlemen?'

The response came thirty minutes later. The men of COBR were just finishing their second drink when the Secretary's red telephone rang. Instead of reaching for it, he merely nodded at the Police Commissioner, who picked it up, listened thoughtfully, then put it down again.

'That was our negotiator,' he said. 'Salim has just phoned to say that he still wants to see the ambassadors. If they're not there in thirty minutes, another hostage will be killed and his or her body thrown onto the street.'

The Secretary sighed again. 'Can your negotiators keep him talking?'

'Probably not much longer.'

'Do you think he'd speak to the Iranian Consul-General by telephone?'

'I doubt it. I think it's too late for that.'

'What about the Imam of London's Central Mosque, as was suggested before?'

'Dr Sayyed Darsh,' the Commissioner said. 'A good man. His friend, the Libyan broadcaster Muhammad Mustafa Ramadan, who regularly attended prayers at the mosque, was gunned down on its steps only a few weeks ago. That incident deeply affected Darsh. For that reason, when Superintendent

Bernard Hodgets of the Anti-Terrorist Squad contacted him, he initially had doubts about whether or not he should go.'

'Why?' the Secretary asked.

'He believes strongly that the mosque exists to serve Muslims in London, whatever their nationality, and that it can only do so if the Imam remains neutral regarding Arab politics. However, the death of his friend, shot down on the steps of the mosque, changed that line of thinking.'

'So he's going to talk to the terrorists?'

'Yes. Hodgets personally collected him from the mosque and took him to Hyde Park Police Station for what turned out to be a very long wait. An hour and a half later, at five o'clock precisely, he was taken from there, escorted through the barricades surrounding the Embassy, and plunked down in the back of a police van, which is where he is now. When the time is ripe, he'll be taken from the police van into the police negotiating room of Alpha Control, now located in the nursery school, where he can talk to Salim by radio phone.'

'Can he say what he wants or has he been briefed?'

'He's been briefed to remind the terrorists of his eminence as an Islamic cleric, then emphasize the immorality of what they're doing in the name of Islam. He is also to reassure them that if they end their resistance and come out peacefully, no harm will come to them and that he will be present at the surrender to ensure that this is so.'

'In other words,' the Secretary said, 'you're not asking him to negotiate or bargain at all. His function is really to convey your terms for surrender.'

'I suppose so,' the Commissioner said.

'And if the Imam also fails to persuade them?'

'Then the SAS Deliberate Assault Plan will commence immediately.'

The Secretary pursed his lips and drummed his fingers once more, then sighed and stood up behind his desk. 'Excuse me, gentlemen, but I have to make a private call.' He walked out of the room. They could hear him murmuring into a phone at the other side of the door. Eventually, the door opened and he returned to take his seat at the other side of the long desk. 'I've just spoken to Mrs Thatcher,' he said, 'and she's approved of our plans for an assault should the forty-five-minute deadline bring us to a negative situation. However, she wishes to remind all concerned that we cannot afford a repeat of Desert One. This operation must be successful.'

'It will be,' the Controller said.

The Secretary nodded. 'May I suggest, then, that we take a short break and meet back here just before six? Personally, I'll spend the time having a light snooze, which should settle the whisky in my stomach and enhance my thought processes.'

'I'll get in touch with my Blue and Red Team leaders,' the Controller said, 'and check that they're prepared.'

'I'll stay here by the telephone and TV,' the Commissioner said, 'and keep in touch with events. If anything happens, I'll call you.'

'You do that,' the Secretary said, then stood up and left the room with the Controller.

Forty-five minutes later, just before six o'clock, the three men, along with representatives of the Foreign Office and the Ministry of Defence, met around the same long table in the same basement room in Whitehall. Learning that the latest deadline had just passed, that no Arab ambassadors had materialized, and that so far there had been no response from the terrorists, every man in the room sensed that the time for negotiation was over.

'If he produces unambiguous evidence that a hostage had been murdered,' the Secretary finally announced, 'the Deliberate

Assault Plan will be put into effect. Please prepare for it.'

Instantly, the Controller phoned the SAS FHA, right next door to the Embassy, to put his Blue and Red Teams onto a ten-minute stand-by.

Before that time was up, however, a phone call from the assistant to Commander Peter Duffy, head of the Anti-Terrorist Squad, informed them that at that very moment the Imam was in the police negotiating room on the second floor of Alpha Control and had just finished speaking to Salim on the radio phone.

Unfortunately, the conversation had been heated and not remotely successful, with the Imam begging Salim to wait until the ambassadors had finished their meeting in the Arab League office in Mayfair and Salim responding that if the ambassadors did not turn up in thirty minutes, he would kill not one but two hostages. When the Imam tried pleading for Salim to think again, the latter slammed his phone down.

Even as the Imam was telling the police that he was 'very disturbed' by Salim's tone of voice, the radio telephone rang again. When one of the negotiators picked it up, he was told by Salim that he had changed his mind and was not going to wait for another thirty minutes. Instead, he would kill a hostage in two minutes.

The Imam rang Salim back to quote the Prophet Muhammad to him, but Salim slammed the receiver down again.

A few seconds later, when the Imam's phone rang again and he picked it up, at first he heard nothing but heavy breathing.

Then he heard the sound of three shots and the line went dead for the last time.

* * *

When the Secretary, who had taken the call from Commander Duffy's assistant, put the phone down, he relayed the story to the rest of the COBR team. Shocked, they hardly knew what to say and instead turned to the television set in the corner. A news flash had just begun. The screen showed the Iranian Embassy for what seemed like an awfully long time. Eventually, the front door was opened and the eyes of a terrorist appeared above a tightly wound *keffia*, peering out cautiously. When the door opened further, two other men could be seen inside, tugging at something heavy, trailing it laboriously across the broken glass on the lobby floor until they reached the entrance. There they turned back into the building, pushed the heavy object out onto the street, then slammed the door.

A corpse lay like a sack of rubbish on the pavement. It was Abbas Lavasani.

13

A small group of nervous policemen dashed to where the murdered press officer lay and hoisted him onto a stretcher. After carrying him back to one of the waiting ambulances, they were able to identify the corpse. The police pathologist, while not yet able to ascertain the exact time of death, was able to establish immediately from the coldness of the body that Lavasani had been dead for hours. He had therefore not been killed by the shots heard just a few minutes ago.

'Either there's another dead body inside,' the pathologist said, 'or Salim has just killed one man and fired those second shots as part of a bluff.'

'It makes no difference now,' the superintendent replied. 'Just a few minutes ago Sir David McNee, our guvnor, telephoned to say he was committing the SAS to action. It's out of our hands now.'

This was true. At seven minutes past seven, the Controller formally took control and hurried back to the SAS FHA at the Royal College of Medical Practitioners, next door to the Embassy. There he found his men already getting into their flame-resistant underwear. The Controller took a seat at the far end of the dormitory while the men continued dressing by putting on their black CRW assault suits with flame-barrier knee and elbow pads; GPV wrap-around soft body armour with hard ceramic composite plates front and back; and specially reinforced, flame-resistant boots. Though the CRW assault suits each had an integral S6 respirator with nose-cap filter, anti-flash hood and goggles, the men would leave these hanging loose until the operation began.

When they finished dressing and were looking, as the Controller thought, suitably sinister, they opened their lockers and withdrew their personal weapons. Sitting on the end of his bed, each man thoroughly cleaned his new Heckler & Koch MP5 sub-machine-gun by removing the magazine, cocking the action and ejecting the 9mm round. He then stripped the weapon and cleaned the working parts by threading the metal beads of the pull-through down the barrel and then oiling the breech-block. This task completed, he reassembled the weapon, replaced the thirty-round magazine, snapped home the cocking handle and set the safety-catch. Much the same process was used for the Browning 9mm High Power handgun, the Remington 870 pump-action shotgun and, in the case of the sniper team led by Sergeant 'Paddy' Shannon, the L42A1 .303-inch bolt-action sniper rifle.

Even as the members of the sniper team were checking and snapping shut their steel bipods, the Red and Blue Teams were checking their webbing, spare ammunition, ISFE, CS gas and MX5 stun grenades. The Heckler & Koch magazines were worn on the left hip, the Brownings on the right, and the spare High Power magazines worn on the left thigh and right wrist, the latter for rapid magazine changes.

As each man finished his preliminary tasks, he sat on the edge of the bed and waited for the others. When the last of the men was done, the Controller stood up to give the final briefing. First he checked his watch and asked all his men to do the same.

'It is now exactly 1915 hours,' he said, 'so please ensure that you all have the same time.' As the men checked their watches, the Controller said: 'The operation commences in five minutes. While we prepare ourselves on the roof, a police negotiator will be keeping the terrorists distracted with promises of a bus to the airport and PC Lock as his driver. You all know your tasks, but let me just summarize again.'

He paused to let those adjusting their watches do so before putting on their black, skin-tight aviator gloves, then continued.

'Red Team is to clear the top half of the building, from second to fourth floors. Blue Team will tackle the lower half from the basement and garden upwards to the first floor, and handle evacuation procedures and the undiplomatic reception on the rear lawn.'

Glancing at Red Team's Staff-Sergeant Harrison and Blue Team's Staff-Sergeant Jock Thompson, he received a nod of acknowledgement from both.

'Once on the roof of Number 16, Red Team's Call Sign Two will lower a frame explosive down the skylight well, lay it as accurately as possible on the window frame, and blow out the skylight at fourth-floor level. Red Team's two groups, Call Sign One and Call Sign Two, each of four men, will then abseil in separate waves from the roof. Two men from Call Sign One will continue down to the ground floor terrace to hack through the back doors and enter with flash-bangs. Call Sign Two will drop to the first-floor balcony and break in through the window with the use of explosives and, if necessary, sledgehammers. To attack the third floor, the remaining two men from Call Sign Two will descend from the roof onto a sub-roof at the rear, known as the lighting area. As all of you men have been allocated your individual tasks, I give this information solely for the benefit of Blue Team, who should know what you're up to.'

'I'm still worried about those windows,' Harrison said. 'I mean, anything we personally recommend has to be tough to get through.'

The Controller waited until the men had stopped laughing. 'The only uncertainty about that concerns the explosive power needed. Each team is therefore being equipped with a special frame charge, approximately the same size as the windows, and packed with a carefully calibrated quantity of plastic explosive. If you plant the frames against the window surround and then explode them, I think they'll do the job.'

He paused to let all of this sink in and to let them ask questions. There were no more questions.

'Blue Team is in charge of the basement at garden level,' the Controller continued, 'along with the ground floor and first floor. Theoretically, all that should be required to get in is an explosive charge to put in the French windows over-looking the ground-floor terrace at the back and a similar bit of surgery on the first-floor front balcony window leading to the Minister's office. As that balcony adjoins this building, access to it shouldn't be a problem. Blue Team, supported by the Zero Delta sniper team facing the building, will also be responsible for firing CS gas canisters into the second-floor rear windows, where we believe the hostages are being held, though they might have been moved by now. The same team is responsible for evacuation of those found inside and will supervise the reception party in the garden afterwards. Any questions?'

There were still no questions, so the Controller looked directly at Sergeant Shannon, leader of the sniper team.

'The sniper teams led by Sergeant Shannon will be divided into two groups and located in a block of flats at the rear of the Embassy and at a camouflaged position in Hyde Park, at the front. When the attack commences they will pump CS gas through the broken windows and also give the assault groups covering fire if and when terrorists emerge from inside the building, either onto the balconies or through the doors. Any questions so far?'

Again there were no questions.

'Once inside the building, you will proceed to your separate tasks as outlined in the merged Immediate Action Plan and Deliberate Assault Plan and rehearsed with the scale model of the building in the Regent's Park Barracks. Resistance is to be met with force and you will shoot to kill. You will not attempt to distinguish between terrorist and hostage. Anyone found inside the building will be manhandled out onto the back lawn, where Blue Team will supervise their reception. This briefing is now at an end, so are there any last questions?'

'Yes,' Sergeant Inman said. 'Who's directing the operation? And from where?'

'The whole operation will be orchestrated by a command group, led by me, operating from a sixth-floor flat overlooking the rear of the Embassy.'

'Out of sight of the journalists,' Jock said.

The Controller grinned. 'I think you've got the picture. Any *more* last questions?' There were none, so he checked his watch, then looked up and said: 'Let's go.'

Even as the negotiator at ground level kept talking to Salim, PC Lock and Sim Harris, keeping them distracted, the twelve-man assault team stood up and marched awkwardly out of the large room, heavily burdened with their weapons, ammunition, break-in tools, abseiling equipment and explosive frames. After making their way up the stairs, the eight members of the Red Team's two groups emerged, via a skylight, in the fading light of evening, onto the roof of the college adjoining the Embassy. The men of the Blue Team took another route, emerging quietly onto the balcony that led from that building to Number 16. There they stopped and waited.

The time was exactly seven-twenty p.m.

Once on the gently sloping roof, the men of the Red Team made their way carefully and silently to the adjoining roof of the Embassy, codenamed 'Hyde Park', and spread out to go about their separate tasks. The four men of Call Sign Two, led by Lance-Corporal Phil McArthur, went immediately to kneel down by the well around the fourth-floor skylight and prepare the explosive frame to be lowered by rope. As they were doing so, the men of Call Sign One went to the rear of the building, overlooking the lawns 80 feet below. There they found the ropes still tied to the chimneys and coiled beneath them, as they had been from the first day of the siege. Slinging their sub-machine-guns over their shoulders, they proceeded to put together the three components of the abseiling equipment by clipping the metal descendeur to the harness, then slipping the recently purchased nylon rope through the descendeur. Standing on the edge of the roof, each man of the abseiling team covered his face with his respirator, hood and goggles, checked that the integral microphones and radio receivers were working, and prepared himself, psychologically and physically, to go over the side.

The abseilers looked like black-clad deep-sea divers.

By now, the four men of Call Sign Two had fixed ropes to the four sides of the large frame explosive and were lowering it down the well to the fourth-floor skylight. When the frame was dangling just above the skylight, they manoeuvred it into position by tugging gently on the ropes, then dropped it carefully over the frame of the skylight so that both frames were more or less matching. When this had been done, the men lay the ends of the four ropes gently on the roof, set the explosive charge with a timer and electronic detonator, then covered their faces with their respirators and joined the other abseilers on the edge of the roof overlooking the rear of the building.

Meanwhile, on the balcony behind protective walls at ground-floor and garden level, the Blue Team, who had already covered their faces with their respirators and goggles, waited with explosives and ladders, each man tuned into the radio frequency that would enable him to strike the moment the attack signal, 'London Bridge', was given.

At that very moment, the attention of Salim and his fellow terrorists was being distracted by the promises being made by the police negotiators. Each time the negotiators called, which they were now doing constantly, first making a promise, then trying to wriggle out of it, Salim would become more agitated and distracted.

The male hostages in the telex room, Room 10, overlooking Princes Gate, and the female hostages in Room 9, on the second floor, were becoming increasingly fearful as the protracted negotiations continued and Salim came close to the end of his tether.

Finally, at the request of the now very disturbed Salim, PC Lock phoned the negotiators again, asking them to get the bus to the Embassy as soon as possible because the terrorists were expecting an attack any minute. When the negotiators smoothly denied that such an attack was on the agenda, Salim wrenched the phone from PC Lock to personally complain that he could hear suspicious noises all around the building.

'No strange noises, Salim,' the police negotiator replied smoothly, glancing at his watch.

At that precise moment, an explosive charge blew away the reinforced skylight roof.

The attack had begun.

14

From the first day of the siege the police had made it perfectly clear that reporters and cameramen, while permitted to view the front of the Embassy, would not be given entry to any area or building affording a view of the rear, where most of the SAS assault would take place.

That evening, an ITN news director, determined not to be obstructed in this way, smooth-talked his way past the police guarding the barricade and was permitted to take a brief stroll along Exhibition Road. Halfway along the road, he stopped to have what appeared to be a casual conversation with the night porter of a block of flats which looked onto Princes Gate. One top-floor flat in particular, he learned, had a good view of the rear of the Embassy and its gardens.

Returning along Exhibition Road, the ITN man thanked the police for their courtesy, then made his way back to the immense press enclosure in Hyde Park, opposite the Embassy.

The following morning, the owner of the top-floor flat in Exhibition Road gave permission to ITN for a TV camera to be installed in his apartment, in the room that overlooked the rear of the Embassy. The problem was getting it in there.

Later that morning, shortly before noon, two men dressed in business suits and carrying suitcases covered in stickers indicating that they had travelled a lot clambered out of a black cab that had stopped at the police barricade at Exhibition Road. The businessmen explained to the police that they had just been abroad and were about to stay with a friend who lived along Exhibition Road.

The police guard kindly informed the cab driver as to how he could enter Exhibition Road by another route. The cabby thanked him and drove off, taking the businessmen with him.

About ten minutes later, the two well-travelled businessmen got out of the cab, paid the driver, and carried their suitcases across the pavement to the building that overlooked the rear of the Embassy.

Like all of the blocks of flats in Exhibition Road at that time, this one was guarded by a policeman. However, when the owner of the top-floor flat told the policeman on duty that he was expecting the callers, they were allowed to enter the building with their well-travelled suitcases.

Once in the top-floor flat, the two 'businessmen' opened the suitcases and withdrew a lightweight ITN TV camera, micro-link equipment and a radio telephone. They set up the camera at the window, then sat behind it and waited patiently.

At seven-twenty p.m. on Day Six of the siege, the ITN news director was back in the press compound, watching his monitor. While most of the other TV cameras were focused on the front of the Embassy, he was receiving a view of the back, from a high vantage point.

As he studied the monitor, he was stunned to see what appeared to be a group of eight sinister, black-clad figures, all wearing respirator masks and carrying weapons and other equipment, emerging via a skylight on the gently sloping roof of the Royal College of Medical Practitioners and making their way stealthily across to the roof of the besieged Embassy.

The formerly secret SAS were about to appear on television all around the world.

15

At the radio signal 'London Bridge' Staff-Sergeant Harrison slipped on the harness and bravely stepped backwards off the Embassy roof to begin his dangerous descent down the 80-foot wall. Hanging out from the wall did not make for a comforting sensation, but Harrison gamely lowered himself down, using the descendeur to control the speed of his drop.

'First man over,' a voice said in his electronic headset. 'Second man over.'

Glancing up, Harrison saw the second Red Team abseiler, Trooper Ken Passmore, about five feet above him, stepping backwards off the edge of the roof, using his booted feet for leverage as his body arched out over the fearsome drop to begin the descent. Satisfied, Harrison glanced down and saw the third-floor window about ten feet below him. Growing more optimistic and excited, he continued his descent, first passing the attic floor, then approaching the balcony window below it.

He had travelled no more than 15 feet when his rope snagged, leaving him dangling just below the attic floor, above the third-floor window.

'Damn!' he exclaimed into his throat mike. 'The bloody thing's seized up!'

'Oh, no!' Ken replied, his voice eerily distorted in Harrison's earphones.

Frustrated, Harrison attempted to unsnag the harness. When he touched it, he almost burned his fingers, and cursed softly.

'What's happened?' Trooper Passmore asked, now dangling a few feet above him, unwilling to drop any further until Harrison moved.

'This new rope,' Harrison said. 'Bloody awful rubbish! It's overheated because of the friction caused by my weight and then ravelled into a knot. Damn!' he muttered, wriggling frantically 65 feet above the rear terrace and lawns, turning this way and that, his feet pressed to the wall, as he tried to disentangle himself. 'I can't unravel the bloody thing!'

Inching lower in his own harness to stop right above him, Ken tried to set him free. For a moment he felt dizzy, looking down at that dreadful drop, but he managed to get a grip on himself and endeavoured again to set Harrison free. Suddenly, by jerking too hard, he made his harness go into a spin and instinctively swung his feet out to prevent himself from crashing into the wall. To his horror, he heard the sound of breaking glass.

'Shit!' he hissed.

Glancing down, he saw that his booted foot had gone through the third-floor window, smashing the pane. The glass broke noisily, some shards raining into the room, others falling all the way down to the terrace, where they were smashed to smithereens, making even more noise.

'Christ!' Harrison groaned in frustration and mounting anger. 'We're compromised already.' Knowing that this was true, and shocked that it had happened so quickly, he snapped into his throat mike: 'Go! Go! Go!'

At that moment, the frame placed over the well skylight exploded with a mighty roar, smashing the glass, shaking the whole building, and causing part of the roof to collapse, the debris raining down on the stairs joining the front and rear second floor.

Simultaneously, Sergeant Shannon's sniper team, Zero Delta, located behind a high wall at the front of the building, began firing CS gas canisters through the broken windows.

From ground positions in front of the Embassy, other members of Zero Delta fired CS gas canisters into the second floor, smashing the windows.

While Harrison and Ken Passmore struggled in their harnesses just above the broken third-floor window, the second pair of abseilers, Inman and Baby Face, dropped down past them, not stopping until they reached the ground-floor terrace. Another pair, Phil and Alan, dropped rapidly to the first-floor balcony window.

Once on the terrace, Inman and Baby Face released themselves from their harnesses. With a swift, expert movement, the staff-sergeant swung his pump-action shotgun into the firing position and blasted the lock off the doors, causing wood splinters and dust to stream out in all directions. Kicking the doors open as Inman dropped to one knee, holding the Remington in one hand and withdrawing his Browning with the other, Baby Face hurled a couple of MX5 stun grenades into the library and rushed in even as they were exploding. Inman followed him, turning left and right, preparing to fire a double tap if he saw any movement.

Though their eyes were protected from the blinding flash by the tinted lenses in their respirators, a combination of condensation on the lenses, natural adjustment to the half-light, and the swirling smoke from the flash-bang made them view the thousands of books on the walls through what seemed like fog.

'Not a soul here,' Inman said as the condensation on his lenses cleared but the smoke continued swirling about them, 'so let's get down the stairs.'

When Inman had slung the Remington over his left shoulder and removed his sub-machine-gun from his right, they hurried out of the library and went straight to the stairs to the cellar. There they were joined by a couple of other Red Team soldiers, emerging from a cloud of swirling smoke like bizarre insect-men from another planet.

'We have to clear the rooms downstairs,' Inman said into his throat mike. 'Was that your brief, too?'

'Yes.'

'Then let's go.'

Though aware that terrorists might be hiding in the cellar and that the entrance could be booby-trapped, they wrenched away the ladders covering the door, tugged the door open, and made their way carefully down the stairs, into the gloom below. Though there was a commotion in the Embassy above them, the cellar was deadly quiet.

'Careful,' Baby Face warned Inman as he took the lead going down, prepared to fire his Browning. 'We can't see a bloody thing down there.'

Agreeing with Baby Face, Inman, when only halfway down, hurled a stun grenade, which exploded with a thunderous crack that ricocheted eerily around the basement. Getting a brief look at the cellar in the brilliant, fluctuating illumination of the flash-bang, he saw no sign of movement and decided that it was safe to descend all the way.

Reaching the corridor at the bottom, he carefully tried the door of the first room but could not open it.

'Locked,' he said. 'They're probably all locked. Well, let's unlock 'em.'

Taking aim with his Browning, he 'drilled' the lock with a couple of 9mm bullets, causing more wood splinters and dust to fly away. When the lock had been blown off, he dropped again to one knee and gave cover as Baby Face threw in a flash-bang and rushed in with the others, aiming left and right, as the grenade exploded and illuminated the room with its brilliant, phosphorescent light.

The room was empty.

'OK,' Inman said, still kneeling by the door, holding his Browning in the firing position, 'let's try the next one.'

They applied the same procedure to the next room, found it empty, and so tried the next one along, which also was empty. They repeated the SOP all the way along the corridor, clearing one room after another, but finding all of them empty.

On entering the last room, however, Inman thought he saw something moving. Instantly, he let off a burst of twenty rounds from his sub-machine-gun. This produced a catastrophic, metallic drumming sound. When the bullets stopped hitting the rolling target, he saw what it was.

'A bloody dustbin!' Baby Face cried out from behind him. 'You've got a quick trigger finger, Sarge!'

'Go screw yourself,' Inman said.

Heading back up the cellar stairs and into reception, they crossed a hallway filled with the smoke from stun grenades and burning curtains. It was also filled with the noise of other members of the assault teams who, having burst into the building from the front and rear, were now clearing the rooms on all floors with a combination of flash-bangs, CS gas grenades, and all the skills they had picked up in CQB training in the 'killing house' in Hereford. The walls and carpets in the hallway and along the landings were singed black and shredded by a combination of grenade explosions and bullets. The smoke was darkening and spreading.

'Christ, what a mess!' Inman said.

He and Baby Face headed for the smoke-wreathed stairs, where they could hear the hysterical voices of female hostages. When they reached the source of the bedlam, they found soldiers forming a line and passing the women down with a speed that left little time for kindness. Most of the women seemed to be in shock, and their eyes were streaming from the CS gas. They were guided down the stairs and through the library, then out onto the lawn. Some were weeping with joy.

Though the Embassy seemed crowded with soldiers, some were still outside. Indeed, on the first-floor balcony, the plan to blast a way through the rear French windows had to be abandoned because of the risk of injuring or killing Staff-Sergeant Harrison, still struggling with Ken Passmore to break free of his harness and now in danger of being burned alive by the flames pouring out through the third-floor window.

'Damn it, Passmore, do something!' Harrison was bawling as both of them twisted in their harnesses, swinging in and out, scorched by the flames and choking in the smoke, vainly trying to release the jammed descendeur. 'This bloody thing is going to be over before we get in there. 'Come on, Passmore! *Do something!*'

'It won't budge!' Ken shouted.

Denied the use of explosive, Alan and Phil, now on the first-floor balcony, smashed through the windows with sledge hammers and threw in flash-bangs. They were releasing themselves from their harnesses and clambering into the office of the chargé d'affaires even as the brilliant flashing from the stun grenades was lighting up the room.

At the front of the Embassy, the Blue Team, caught in the golden light of the early evening and in full view of the stunned reporters and TV cameras in Hyde Park, clambered from the adjoining balcony and along the ornate ledge until they reached the heavily reinforced windows of the Minister's office.

Glancing sideways as he made his way along the ledge, Jock saw the police cordon in the street below and the press enclosure across the road, where a lot of TV cameras raised on gantries were focused on the Embassy and, it seemed, on him. Startled, he looked away and continued his careful advance until he came up behind the first two men.

Danny Boy and Bobs-boy, being the first at the window, saw Sim Harris staring at them in disbelief from the other side of the glass.

'Get down!' Danny Boy bawled through his respirator. 'Stand back and get down!'

Though clearly stunned, the sound recordist did as he was told, standing away from the window to let Danny Boy and Bobs-boy, who were being covered by Jock and GG, place the frame charge over the window.

While they were still putting their plastic strip charges in place, a terrorist armed with a Polish-made Skorpion W263 sub-machine-gun appeared at the second-floor window of the telex room immediately above them. The man flung the window open and hurled something down.

'Grenade!' Jock bawled.

However, clearly the terrorist had forgotten to draw the detonating pin and the grenade bounced harmlessly away. That was his first mistake. His second was to expose himself at the window long enough to become a target for the SAS sniper, Sergeant Shannon, hiding across the road in Hyde Park. Aiming along the telescopic sight of his bipod-mounted L42A1 .303-inch bolt-action sniper rifle, Paddy hit the man with a single round. The terrorist staggered back, dropping his gun, then disappeared from view.

As the frame charge blew in the first-floor window, filling the air with flying glass, Jock hurled in a stun grenade. The exploding flash-bang ignited the curtains and filled the room with smoke.

Suddenly, Sim Harris reappeared, emerging ghostlike from the smoke and looking gaunt. Carefully approaching the window, he leaned out to stare disbelievingly at the SAS men in their black CRW suits, body armour, respirators and balaclava helmets.

'What . . .?'

'Get the hell out of there,' Jock said. Ignoring the flames, he and Danny Boy grabbed Harris by the shoulders and roughly hauled him out through the smashed window, onto the balcony, where they pressed him down onto his hands and knees. 'Stay here and keep your head down,' Jock told him, 'until you're told to do otherwise. Wait till someone comes for you.'

As Jock and the other three Blue Team members scrambled through the window, a revitalized Harris sat up on his haunches and shouted excitedly after them: 'Go on, lads! Get the bastards!'

By now, Phil and Alan, of the Red Team, had made their way across the smoke-wreathed stairs of the first floor. There they heard shouts from an adjoining office – that of the Minister's secretary.

Rushing in, they found the police hostage, PC Lock, struggling violently with a bearded terrorist who was holding an

RGD5 hand-grenade in one hand and a Skorpion W263 Polish sub-machine-gun in the other. Though clearly in pain, PC Lock was wrestling gamely with the bearded terrorist, holding his right wrist to prevent him from hurling the grenade and falling with him over the furniture in a noisy mêlée. Lock had drawn his own .38 Smith & Wesson revolver and was trying to put it to the terrorist's head with his free hand, but either he just could not manage it or he was reluctant to kill at close quarters.

As the two men wrestled furiously, Phil grabbed Lock with his free hand and jerked him away from the terrorist, whom he recognized instantly from photographs as the leader, Salim.

'Trevor, leave off!' he bawled.

As Phil turned away from Lock, Salim, who had almost fallen over, was trying to regain his balance. Before he could do so, the lance-corporal fired a burst of automatic fire at his head and chest and his fellow SAS man, Alan, did the same, both using their MP5 sub-machine-guns. Hit by fifteen bullets, Salim was thrown backwards like an epileptic having a fit and smashed down through the furniture to lie face up in the rubble on the floor.

He died instantly, becoming the martyr he had long dreamed of being.

Heading across the first-floor landing towards the rear of the building, past burning curtains, through pockets of smoke, and brushing against other hurrying, bawling SAS soldiers, Phil and Alan tried the door to the Ambassador's office.

'Locked!' Phil said into his throat mike.

He was raising his MP5 to blow the door open when it was opened from within and he found himself face to face with a youthful terrorist armed with a Browning.

Before Phil could fire again, Alan, just behind him and to the right, fired a short, savage burst from his MP5. The terrorist screamed and staggered back into the room, then Phil threw a stun grenade after him. The combined blast and flash threw the terrorist even further back and made him stumble blindly. Alan fired a second time, making the terrorist scream out again, but instead of falling he gained the strength of the desperate and staggered deeper into the smoke-filled room, eventually disappearing.

'Shit!' Alan cried, squinting to see through the condensation on his respirator lenses, as well as through the smoke.

'He's still alive, he's wounded and he's desperate,' Phil said to his mate. 'And he's got a weapon.'

'We can't see a damned thing in there,' Alan said.

'We can't let that bastard get away.'

'So let's go in after him.'

They advanced into the room, but as they entered the smoke, Phil felt himself choking.

'Shit!' he spluttered. 'It's CS gas and it's penetrated my respirator. I'm choking to death. I've got to get out of here.'

Coughing harshly, he staggered outside, ripped his respirator off, breathed the air, which was filled with the less noxious smoke from burning curtains, then placed his respirator back over his face and took deep, even breaths.

'Anybody got a light?' Alan shouted into his throat mike, now trapped in the dense smoke in the room and not able to see a thing.

Jock, on his way up from the ground floor, heard Alan's cry for help. Hurrying up the stairs, he found Phil about to re-enter the smoke-filled room.

'Let me go first,' Jock said. 'I've got a torch bolted to my MP5.'

Turning on the torch and holding the MP5 as if about to fire from the hip, he advanced into the room with Phil beside him. When he moved the sub-machine-gun left and right, up and down, the thin beam of light from the torch illuminated the darkness and, eventually, Alan.

Not wishing to speak, Alan used a hand signal to indicate that he thought the terrorist was hiding in the far left corner of the room. Nodding, Jock moved towards the trooper, waited until he had fallen in beside him and Phil, then led them carefully through the dense smoke, aiming the barrel of the MP5 left and right, up and down, lighting up the darkness and, more dangerously, pinpointing his own position to the hidden enemy.

No shots were fired at him and eventually, in that thin beam of light, Jock, Phil and Alan saw a hand, then a face . . . and then a Browning.

The wounded terrorist was sprawled on a large sofa near the bay window overlooking the garden. He was covered in blood. When he weakly took aim with the pistol, his hand shook and wavered uncertainly from left to right.

The three SAS men all fired their Heckler & Koch MP5 sub-machine-guns simultaneously, stitching the terrorist repeatedly, throwing him into convulsions, making him writhe dementedly and shake like a rag doll in the hands of an angry child. Pieces of torn upholstery, foam-filling and feathers exploded from what had been a luxurious sofa, only to drift back down like snow on his bloody remains.

This time, hit by twenty-one bullets, the terrorist did not survive.

At the rear of the building, on the third floor, some Red Team members were still in serious trouble. On the outside wall, just below Ken Passmore, Staff-Sergeant Harrison remained trapped in his abseiling harness, dangling and kicking ever more frantically 75 feet above the rear terrace. To make matters worse, flames from the fire were now roaring out of the general office window and starting to burn up his legs. To avoid being burnt even worse, and also to avoid choking in the billowing smoke, he had been kicking himself away from the wall, as if on a swing. However, this helped very little, for each time he swung back to the wall, he found himself in the smoke and flames again.

'Cut me loose!' he finally bellowed in desperation.

'Jesus, boss, I . . .'

'Just do it!'

Aware that if he cut the nylon rope, Harrison could plunge to a brutal death, Ken was reluctant to do so. Nevertheless, with the fire in the third-floor room growing stronger and the flames licking out through the window to coil up on the wind and attack the staff-sergeant, Ken saw that he had no choice. He therefore withdrew his Fairburn-Sykes commando knife from its sheath and, with a great deal of effort, being himself trapped in mid-air and scorched by the flames, hacked through the nylon cord snagged in the descendeur.

'Any second now!' he bellowed as the last threads were shredded.

Harrison fell through the flames onto the balcony. Burnt and blistered, but free at last, he smashed the third-floor window with his small, belt-held sledgehammer, hurled in some stun grenades, and swung himself into the smoke-filled interior of the large general office, where, according to their briefing, most of the hostages were held.

The room was empty. It was also locked, barricaded and piled high with inflammable material that had just been ignited by the flash-bangs.

Nevertheless, when Ken had followed him into the room, Harrison advanced blindly with his trooper through the dense smoke and flames until he reached the locked door, which he recognized only after tracing it with his fingertips. Already in a temper because of his bad start, he blew the locks apart with a couple of shots from his Browning. The locks gave way in a hail of dust and wood splinters, but the doors, barricaded from the other side, remained firmly locked.

'I'm going to try another route,' Ken said.

Retreating to the balcony, he clambered across to an adjoining window ledge. From there he could see inside the room, where a terrorist was striking matches to set fire to paper piled up against the wall. Before the terrorist could look up and see him perched on the ledge, Ken smashed the window and hurled a stun grenade. The explosion shook the terrorist and temporarily blinded him; so, although he managed to raise his pistol to fire, he fled from the room instead.

Still perched on the window ledge, Ken aimed his MP5 and fired from the hip.

The weapon jammed.

Cursing, Ken drew his Browning, clambered off the ledge, dropped into the room, and went after the terrorist, the former mechanic Shakir Sultan Said. He lost the terrorist temporarily in the smoke, but then saw him racing into what Ken knew, from his frequent rehearsals with the plywood model of the Embassy, was the telex room, where most of the male hostages were held. It was off to the right across the landing, which was covered in smoke.

Unseen by Ken, another terrorist, Shakir Abdullah Fadhil, the group's second in command, had just run into the room with Badavi Nejad and Makki Hounoun Ali, when Said, fleeing the trooper, also reached it. Seeing the unarmed male

153

hostages huddling fearfully together in the corner of the room, Fadhil swept them with a burst of automatic fire from his Skorpion W263 sub-machine-gun, causing them to turn into a shuddering mass of bloodstained protoplasm in which, for the moment, it was impossible to tell who had been hit and who spared.

Inspired by this gross act, Badavi Nejad emptied his .38 Astra revolver into them as well.

The Embassy doorman, Abbas Fallahi, at least knew that he had been hit – and saved. Checking for wounds as he crouched with the other frightened hostages, some of whom were now covered in blood, he discovered that he had only been saved from death because a 50-pence coin in the right pocket of his jacket had deflected the bullet. Fallahi was just uttering profound thanks for his salvation when a canister of smoke, fired from the other side of Princes Gate, smashed through the window of the telex room, hitting him and knocking him to the ground as the room filled with smoke.

Having helped in the attack, Badavi Nejad dropped his pistol in panic and wriggled his way in amongst the surviving hostages. As he was doing so, Fadhil was throwing his sub-machine-gun through the window and emptying his pockets of ammunition. Said, being the last to enter, could think of nothing to do other than stand in the smoke-filled room with his finger crooked inside the pin of a grenade.

Ken, now being followed by Harrison, heard the shots and screams of the victims as he charged towards the telex room. Even as he was rushing towards that sound, some of the surviving hostages were wriggling away from the group on the floor, grabbing the discarded weapons and ammunition of the terrorists and throwing them out of the window into the street below.

With his MP5 in his left hand and his Browning in his right, Ken reached the telex room, kicked the door open and immediately turned the corner, crouching, gun raised in a classic CQB stance. When he saw the figure to his left, grenade in hand, he quickly fired a single round at the head. Entering Said's skull just below the left ear, the 9mm bullet exited through his right temple, blowing out blood, bone and brains, and killing him instantly.

Emerging from the general office and following the sound of shooting, Harrison, still in a raging temper, soon reached the telex room, where he found one dead terrorist, one dead hostage and two badly wounded men.

'Who's a terrorist?' he heard himself bawling angrily before he could stop himself. 'Who's a terrorist?'

Receiving no reply, he grabbed the first English-looking person he could find and jerked him roughly to his feet.

'I'm not a terrorist. I'm Ron . . .'

Before the caretaker could say anything, Harrison, despite the dreadful pain of his burns, threw him roughly across the room towards the door where, he knew, other SAS men would manhandle him, none too gently, down the stairs, through the library and out onto the rear lawn where, like all the others, terrorist and hostage alike, he would be laid face down on the ground and trussed up like a chicken.

'Who's a terrorist?' Harrison shouted again, hardly recognizing the sound of his own voice. 'Who's a damned terrorist?' An Iranian face looked up from the smoke-wreathed, blood-soaked group on the floor. 'You!' Harrison bawled. 'Who are you?'

'The cultural . . .'

'Who are the terrorists?'

155

Jock and GG burst into the telex room as the Iranian on the floor pointed tentatively at two men sitting with their backs to the room and their hands on the wall. Before Harrison or anyone else could say anything, Jock and GG fired a sustained burst at the two men, hitting one in the head and the other in the neck and pelvis, punching both of them forward face first into the wall, where they slid shuddering down to the floor, leaving a trail of blood.

'Stay there!' Harrison bawled at the others. 'Don't move unless instructed!' He turned to Jock and GG. 'Let's check them quickly for weapons, then get them out of here. Keep your eyes peeled for terrorists.'

The first thing they did was separate the wounded and the dead from those still untouched. Among the hostages attacked by the terrorists, Dr Afrouz, the chargé d'affaires, had been hit by two bullets, one of which passed through his right thigh; Ahmed Dagdar, the medical adviser, had been savagely wounded by six bullets; and another member of staff, Ali Samad-Zadeh, had been killed outright.

As nothing could be done for the last-named – or indeed for the dead terrorist already identified as Shakir Sultan Said – GG, as a medical specialist, temporarily staunched the wounds of the two wounded hostages with field dressings. Satisfied that he had done all he could here, he left the room with Jock to take part in the evacuation of the building and the 'undiplomatic reception' outside on the back lawn.

16

Even before the survivors were moved out of the choking atmosphere of the telex room, Harrison, now cooled down, and Ken, still level-headed, tried to identify the 'worms' who had wriggled their way into the huddled mass on the floor.

The hostages, some with eyes streaming from CS gas, others covered in the blood of those killed or wounded, all dishevelled, most in shock, were bundled out one by one, then passed by the chain of Red Team soldiers along the corridor with its smouldering curtains, bullet-peppered walls and blackened carpets, down the smoke-filled stairs, across a hallway reeking of stinging CS gas, all the way out through the relatively untouched library and onto the rear lawn, where darkness was falling.

The first 'worms' were easily identified because they had forgotten to remove their green combat jackets. Others, however, had had the sense to do so and were marched with the genuine hostages down the stairs to the lawn, where the female hostages were already face down on the grass, their hands and feet tethered.

One of them did not make it that far. As the last of the hostages was being taken from the telex room, the Red Team searched the suspects and were put on their guard by two who seemed too wary and alert to be hostages.

'If they're hostages I'm Donald Duck,' Ken said.

'And I'm Mickey Mouse,' Harrison replied, increasingly impressed by the trooper. 'Let's have a talk with them.'

Leaving both men to the last, they waited until the other hostages had left, then spoke first to the smaller, more nervous of the two suspects.

'Lie down,' Harrison told him.

The man did so, stretching his arms above his head without being asked, like someone used to the experience.

'Who are you?' Harrison asked, standing over him and aiming his MP5 at his spine.

'Student. I am student.'

'I'll bet you are,' Harrison murmured. Stepping away, but keeping the suspect covered, he nodded to Ken. 'Search him,' he said.

The trooper did so, running his hands over the suspect's body, then pushing his legs open and inspecting his crutch. There he saw the glint of metal – something that resembled a pistol magazine – and then a holster tangled up in the trousers.

'Well, well,' Ken said dryly, 'what have we here, then?'

Suddenly drawing his arms in towards his body, the suspect started rolling over onto his back. Before he could do so, Harrison fired a short burst into his back, killing him instantly, and punching him belly down again, onto the floor.

When Ken turned the body over, he found a hand-grenade as well as the magazine for a .38 Astra revolver. 'Little bastard,' he said. Quickly frisking the body, he came up with an Iraqi identity card, the details of which he read aloud to Harrison. 'Makki Hounoun Ali, twenty-five, a Baghdad mechanic.'

'A mechanic who carries a .38 revolver,' Harrison replied. 'Pull the other one, darling.'

Harrison turned to grin at Ken, but when he did so, he saw the trooper and his double, standing almost side by side, though one was slightly overlapping the other, slightly transparent, like a ghost.

At first Harrison was shocked, thinking he was hallucinating. Then he realized that his burns on his legs were hurting dreadfully and that the pain was causing him double vision. Though the pain remained agonizing, he heaved a sigh of relief.

'I'm not feeling too good,' he confessed. 'I think I'd better go out and see the medics. Can you handle the rest of this?'

'Sure, boss.'

'Good man,' Harrison said.

He turned away to leave the room, felt nauseous, saw two of everything, then fell down through a spinning, light-flecked darkness into oblivion.

Shocked, Ken leaned over him, checked that he was still breathing and realized that he had passed out from a combination of pain and exhaustion. Using the throat mike on his respirator, he called up the special medical team, asking for a stretcher.

While the normally sharp-eyed trooper was thus engaged, the second suspect, Fadhil, the second in command, slipped away into the smoke and gathering darkness, where he mingled with the last of the freed hostages on their way down the stairs.

The members of the Blue Team who had cleared the basement and ground floor had met up with the other members of the Blue and Red Teams from the upper storeys to form the chain along which the hostages were now passed or – as some would later have it – thrown from hand to hand down the stairs and out through the library, then onto the lawn to be trussed up for more intensive body searches and interrogation. Brutal though this would have appeared to the uninitiated, it sprang from the soldiers' fear that the terrorists might have hidden an explosive charge on one of their own people or on a hostage, as their final response to this attack.

Formerly of the Blue Team, now part of the Red, Sergeant Inman was standing in the chain, next to Baby Face, about halfway down the main staircase linking the first floor to the ground, when he heard the sounds of what he thought was a scuffle above him and shouted a warning to the Red Team members up on the landing.

To his relief, it was only the last of the hostages stumbling down the stairs, most of them looking frightened and dishevelled, their eyes streaming from CS gas. Then Inman, with eighteen years of hard experience behind him, saw a face that was calculating rather than scared. That was all he needed to see.

'That one's a terrorist!' he bawled.

The sound of his voice cut through the fearful atmosphere like a knife as those dark eyes under an Afro hairstyle stared down in panic. Instantly recognized as a terrorist by his green combat jacket – Inman's outburst had merely confirmed it for the doubtful – the man was struck on the back of the head by the butt of Phil's MP5. After crying out and stumbling forward a few steps, he advanced down the broad stairs almost at the crouch, his hands over his head as he was punched and kicked down by the chain of soldiers.

When he drew level with Inman, the latter saw a Russian fragmentation grenade with the detonator cap protruding from his hand. Without thinking twice, the sergeant removed the MP5 from his shoulder and slipped the safety-catch to automatic. Unfortunately, his own mates were in the line of fire and prevented him from shooting at the terrorist. Frustrated, he raised the weapon above his head and brought the stock down on the back of the Arab's neck, hitting him as hard as he could. The terrorist's head snapped backward.

At that moment, the four Red Team members at the top of the rubble-strewn stairs opened fire simultaneously, emptying their magazines into the terrorist as he fell. First convulsing wildly in the murderous hail of bullets, then rolling down the stairs and coming to rest on the floor, the terrorist spasmed and vomited blood. He then opened his hand to release the RGD5 grenade, which rolled a short distance across the floor and then came to a stop, making a light drumming noise on the tiles.

Luckily its pin was still in its housing.

After hurrying down the stairs to frisk the dead man, Inman withdrew a wallet containing an identity card and some other papers.

'Shakir Abdullah Fadhil,' he pronounced after studying the items in his hands. 'Also known as Feisal. Aged twenty-one, born in Baghdad, and another Ministry of Industry official. I'll bet he was.' Pocketing the identity card and papers, which he would pass on to Military Intelligence, Inman leaned over the body to make a rough count of the bloody wounds. Straightening up again, he said to the soldiers still on the stairs: 'There are almost forty bullet holes in that bastard and he deserves every one of them.' Grinning, he added a few last words: 'And the pubs haven't closed yet.' Then the sergeant sauntered through the library and out onto the rear lawn.

For some time after that incident, more shots echoed throughout the building as the SAS men blasted away locks to check other rooms. The fires that started with the burning curtains had now engulfed the top of the building and the smoke was forming black clouds that drifted all the way down.

The integral UHF radio headsets in the men's respirators crackled into life as the Controller informed them that the building was ablaze and must be abandoned.

'The Embassy is clear. I repeat: the Embassy is clear.'

Outside on the lawn, most of the hostages were lying face down on the grass, their feet and hands bound. Those remaining were being processed the same way.

Sim Harris, also bound hand and foot, but grateful to have escaped with his life, was asked to identify any surviving terrorists. There was only one left. Identified by PC Lock and Harris, as well as the other survivors, he was Badavi Nejad, also known as Ali Abdullah. Dragged roughly to his feet by Inman and Baby Face, he was handed over to the police and driven away without delay.

Sim Harris, as he lay on the rear lawn, listening to the complaints of another trussed-up hostage, said: 'Think yourself lucky.'

Inman heard the remark. Grinning, he turned to Baby Face and said: 'Now doesn't that make it all worth while?'

'Go screw yourself, Sarge,' Baby Face said with a grin. Then he walked away, heading back to the FHA next door to meet up with his mates.

17

The SAS assault on the Iranian Embassy at 16 Princes Gate, London, ended approximately fifty minutes after it began.

Fifteen minutes later, back in the Forward Holding Area in the Royal College of Medical Practitioners, next door to the Embassy, those who had taken part in the operation stripped off their CRW assault kit, packed it into their civilian holdalls, and wrapped their Heckler & Koch MP5 sub-machine-guns in plastic bags to be taken away for examination, this being the first time they had been used by the Regiment.

'The shortest battle I ever fought,' Jock said. 'It must be some kind of record.'

'Right,' Harrison replied. 'Fifteen minutes to clear the building, thirty-five minutes to check the premises and conduct an undiplomatic reception for the poor sods we rescued – won't they love us? – then another fifteen minutes to pack up our gear and move out of the FHA. Sixty-five minutes from start to finish, then back to Hereford. Not bad at all, mate.'

'We'll be in the *Guinness Book of Records*,' Jock said. 'Take my word for it.'

'No, we won't,' Harrison replied, being more of a realist than his Scottish friend, 'because we don't exist. At least, not officially.'

'We *didn't* exist,' Jock emphasized, 'but we certainly do now. We're all TV stars.'

'Then God help us, Jock.'

Just before leaving the college to enter the Avis vans that would take them back to their temporary bashas in Regent's Park Barracks, the SAS men received a visit from the Home Secretary, William Whitelaw, who, with tears in his eyes, thanked them for all they had done.

Approximately two and a half hours after the siege had ended, the Commanding Officer of 22 SAS handed back control of the cleared, though badly damaged Embassy to the Deputy Assistant Commissioner of the Metropolitan Police, thus officially ending SAS involvement.

Out of a total of twenty-six hostages taken in the Embassy, five had been released before the assault, nineteen had been rescued, and only two had died, neither killed by the SAS.

The survivors included the caretaker, Ron Morris, and PC Lock, who was awarded the George Medal.

There were no SAS casualties at all.

Five of the SAS men were personally decorated by the Queen. Four received the Queen's Gallantry Medal, and one received the George Medal.

Those facts reflected great credit on the SAS and, combined with the fact that most of the operation had been viewed by television viewers worldwide, made theirs, virtually overnight, the most renowned regiment in modern military history.

The sight of those sinister, hooded, well-armed, black-clad figures entering a smoke-filled building in the middle of London captured the public imagination and turned the SAS, formerly anonymous, into the focus of relentless public and media scrutiny, for good or for ill.

The deterrent effect of Operation Pagoda was evident from the fact that no similar event occurred in the United Kingdom for more than a decade afterwards. That single SAS operation had, in effect, protected London from a particularly odious brand of international terrorism.

Ironically, after the inquest and the trial of the surviving terrorist, there was media criticism of the force used by the SAS. The official response from Hereford was that the object of the operation was to rescue hostages and that to do so in a burning building reported to have been wired for a 'Doomsday' explosion did not leave the assault force any other option.

Though the Regiment then tried to sink back into its former anonymity, concentrating on intelligence gathering and security in the absence of a major military task, it never fully regained its former, generally preferred anonymity.

Indeed, twelve months later, at a private bar in Hereford, some of those who had taken part in the Embassy siege could still be heard excitedly discussing it while drinking their beer and Scotch.

'My first time on TV,' Jock Thompson said. 'When I clambered across that first-floor balcony, I almost found myself posing.'

'You should have blown the press a kiss,' Phil McArthur told him. 'They would have loved you for that.'

'A disaster,' someone else said out of the blue, having just arrived, unexpected, at the bar. 'They should have kept the press out of there altogether. That's *my* opinion.'

All those in the small group stared in surprise at the quietly spoken Baby Face, who looked like an innocent schoolboy but was known to be deadly.

'A disaster?' Alan Pyle repeated, as if not hearing right. 'Are you kidding us, Baby Face?'

'This Regiment's supposed to work in secrecy,' Baby Face informed him, 'and that means we should never be seen on TV, discussed on the radio, or even read about in the papers. All that's gone since the Princes Gate siege and I think it's a bad thing.'

'Aren't you proud of what you did there?' Corporal George Gerrard asked. 'I mean, what we all did there was something pretty special, so you shouldn't resent the world knowing about it.'

'I just mean . . .' But Danny could not explain it. Even back home, in Kingswinford, where he was willing to admit that he had fought in Northern Ireland, he refused to let anyone know that he had been one of the sinister, black-clad figures on the roof of that Embassy. He was certainly proud of what he had done, but he disliked the way the operation had been blown up by the papers. The SAS had always taken pride in staying in the background, but the Iranian Embassy affair had destroyed its anonymity and even made it notorious. Baby Face hated the thought of that.

'I loved it,' Sergeant Inman confessed. 'It made me feel like a star. I used to feel like a dick-head, just another faceless soldier, but now everywhere I go, when I say I'm in the SAS, women cream at the sight of me, men burn up with envy, and everyone wants to know what we get up to. I think I'm going to write a bestseller about it.'

'Better be quick,' Jock said. 'You might have left it too late. That Trooper Andrew Winston – the big black bastard from D Squadron – has already had some of his bloody awful poems published and now thinks he's Tolstoy.'

'Who's Tolstoy?' Ken asked.

'I know him,' Bobs-boy Quayle said. 'Not Tolstoy – Andrew Winston. He fought in Defa and Shershitti, in Oman, in the mid-1970s. He's a fucking good bloke.'

'Good man or not, he's getting his poems published,' Jock said, 'and he claims he's going to write about the Regiment and make his name overnight.'

'It just goes to show what this Regiment's becoming,' Inman muttered, licking his moist lips. 'There was a time when no one knew we existed, but Princes Gate changed all that.'

'Not for the best,' Baby Face said. 'I'm certain of that. As for you, Sarge' – he looked straight at Inman – 'you wouldn't be thinking of wasting your time writing if you had another decent war to fight.'

'I think you're right,' Inman replied, 'but alas, there won't be another war. Those days are gone for good.'

'God help us,' Jock said.

That conversation took place during a celebratory drink in the Paludrine Club at the SAS base, Bradbury Lines, Hereford, on 5 May 1981, precisely one year after the Princes Gate siege. Eleven months later, on 2 April 1982, a garrison of British Royal Marines guarding Port Stanley, capital of the Falkland Islands, was forced to surrender to Argentinian forces. Three days later, a Royal Navy Task Force sailed for the Falklands. The very same day, but in secret, D Squadron, 22 SAS, flew out of England on a C-130 Hercules transport plane, bound for Ascension Island and another war.